Detecting Fear

A Collection Of Mystery, Suspense & Intrigue

FIRST EDITION

Shannon Hollinger

DETECTING FEAR: A COLLECTION OF MYSTERY, SUSPENSE & INTRIGUE.

First edition published 2021.

Scene Of The Crime Publications

ISBN: 978-0-578-85687-2

Editing, book cover design and formatting by: Shannon Hollinger

Table of Contents

Detecting Fear

Edgar may have been caught, but his fun isn't over yet. He shrugs his shoulders, trying to relieve the intense discomfort in his arms, but it's tough with them shackled behind his back. He gives one feeble tug against the cuffs, shifts his weight in the hard metal chair, and then turns his attention elsewhere.

The table before him is covered in mug rings of various ages, some dormant and covered in a thick layer of dust, others still actively sticky, catching the light with a gooey sheen. Edgar wants to touch the sticky rings, to feel the tackiness adhere to his fingertips. He licks his lips, thinking about the sensation, when the hairs on his arms twitch, sensing the disturbance in the air as the door opens. His eyes move toward the thudding steps, a pair of boots entering his field of vision. Large, black, well worn, with something smeared on the left toe.

"What's your name?"

He stares, transfixed, at the soiled boot.

"Hey, I asked your name."

"Sometimes I have no name," he answers without thinking, his eyes never leaving the boot.

"Don't get smart with me, bud." It's growled in his face, Edgar's neck snapping back as his shoulders are pinned to the chair by oversized hands. A foul wave of coffee breath slaps him in the face. "You're in a world of trouble. What you did . . ."

"What did I do?" he asks, finally tearing his gaze from the boot, raising his eyes slowly up to meet those of the hulk before him. The corner of his mouth twitches into the beginning of a grin.

"Don't even try me, buddy," Detective Shaw sneers, giving the man's shoulders a final shove as he turns away.

"What. Did. I. Do." Each word is said slowly, purposefully. "Tell me, detective. Tell me what I did?" he taunts. He watches the detective's back muscles stiffen under his shirt. "Was it bad?" he whispers. "Did you like it?" he hisses.

Detective Shaw spins around, catching himself before he swings. Composing himself, he studies the man in front of him. Small, non-descript, almost feminine in his gracile form. Ordinary clothes, a navy polo shirt tucked into khakis, brown leather loafers and belt. A black watch with a plastic band is wrapped around his tiny wrist. His face is clean shaven, skin smooth, not young, not old. Plain brown hair, medium length.

Everything about the guy is generic. There is nothing to raise an alarm. Nothing to make anyone take notice. He could be the man in line next to you at the grocery store, and you would never suspect you were standing beside a brutal killer. It didn't seem fair.

"Tell me detective," the man asks in a calm, inquisitive tone. "What is it that you are most afraid of?"

"I'm not here to answer your questions. Are you ready to talk, or not?"

"Can we talk about what that is, there, on your shoe?" Edgar looks pointedly at the smear on the boot.

Detective Shaw looks down, sees the mess on his foot, curses. The optical membrane is hardening on his boot as it dries.

"What's the matter detective?" Edgar calls after him as he hurries out of the room.

*****

Shuddering in disgust, Detective Shaw braces a hand against the wall, facing the uniformed officer approaching from down the hall.

"We get an ID on this sicko yet, Frank?" he barks.

"Yes, sir," Frank says, handing a printout to the detective.

Detective Shaw takes the paper, skims it. He turns around, staring through the small window in the door at the man seated inside. "What that guy did . . ."

"I heard it was bad, sir," Frank offers.

"Bad doesn't even begin to describe it. I've never been to a scene like that before. It didn't even look like it could have been done by a man's hands. I never would have looked at a guy like the one sitting in there and imagined him capable of such carnage."

The detective shakes his head sadly and looks at the paper in his hand again. "This says here that the family has an eight-year-old boy?"

"That's right, sir."

"There wasn't a little boy at the scene. You guys find any sign of the kid?"

"No, sir, he's still missing. They have an APB and an Amber Alert out for him now. Detective Mills and a couple of the techs are trying to trace the perp's steps, but they haven't come up with anything yet."

"So, he's still out there?"

"Guess so."

Detective Shaw takes a deep breath to compose himself. Damn. He has a nephew around that age, his sister's kid. The cases with children are always harder to work.

As usual, he hopes that they find the kid somewhere safe and sound, but this time, what he hopes for the most is that the kid hadn't had to see the rest of his family in the condition Shaw had. He couldn't imagine being a kid and trying to live with that memory. Hell, he didn't even know how he was going to live with it yet. Putting his hand on the door handle, he squeezes it as if it were the perp's scrawny neck and steps back inside the room.

Edgar looks at him with a leering grin. "How ya feeling, detective?" he asks.

Detective Shaw ignores the question, settling himself on the corner of the table, facing Edgar. He crosses his arms over his chest, keeping the man focused tightly under a steady glare. Edgar shifts uncomfortably.

"I see you forgot to clean your shoe," he says. "I could help you with that, if you'd like. I could use a snack."

Detective Shaw remains silent and continues to stare the man down.

Edgar severs the gaze and focuses on the soiled boot, transfixed by the way the ends of the membranes are curling into tendrils as they dry. It reminds him of the vine that grew behind the shed in his backyard when he was a kid, the one he used to hide his projects under. The detective kicks his chair, the sudden jolt breaking his daze. Edgar looks up at him, momentary disoriented, his trance broken.

"Where's the kid?" Shaw asks.

Edgar's lips curl into a menacing grin. "Oh yeah," he says, his eyes meeting Shaw's once again. "I forgot about him. He's fun."

"Where is he?"

"Oh, he's around. A little here, a little there, you know how it goes. His whole family seems to have suffered from a predisposition to fall to pieces."

Shaw feels his stomach sour, a roiling that ransacks his bowels with brutal force. "We know that's not true," Shaw lies. "We know the kid's still alive. You can make this as easy or as hard on yourself as you want."

"I never said he was dead," Edgar counters. His smile widens as he sees the implication of his words dawn on Shaw. "Like I said, he's a fun little guy. He likes to play. A lot. But he's probably starting to feel pretty lonely about now. What time is it, detective?"

"Where is he?" Shaw repeats.

"What do I get if I tell you?"

"To keep your health."

"Oh now, detective, that's not very nice. What did I ever do to you?"

"You gave me a headache. Now talk."

"What are you afraid of, detective? What is it that makes you truly scared?"

"Knowing that scumbags like you think they're smart."

"Ouch. My feelings are truly hurt. What's the time, detective?"

"I'm not interested in chatting. I just want to know where the kid is."

"Are you sure? Are you really sure you can handle that? I mean, I can see that today's already been a big day for you."

Detective Shaw ignores the words, keeping his expression emotionless. He lowers his face even with Edgar's, their eyes only inches apart. He can smell the sweat off the man's skin, mingled with the fading scent of his shaving cream. His eyes bore through the man before him like a drill through drywall.

A knock on the door intrudes.

Frank sticks his head through the door. "We got a lead off some debris from the tires, sir. Crime scene recovered some trace elements that they've pinpointed to a couple of old mines to the west. I wanted to let you know, see if you wanted to come with or not?"

Shaw watches Edgar's reaction, sees a hint of surprise in the man's eyes.

"Yeah," he says, straightening up. "There's nothing going on here." Turning to leave, he pauses as Edgar speaks.

"Detective," the man in the chair says. "I did take the boy out to a mine. The old Stockton mine off of 95. But he's not there anymore. He wasn't scared of the dark, so we had to find a new place to play."

"And where would that be?" Detective Shaw asks without turning around.

"Is it 2:30 yet?"

Shaw waves the uniform out of the room before facing the man, the look in his eyes lethal. "Where did you take the kid?"

"I took him to Devil's Peak," Edgar says. "We hiked all the way up until we were on that narrow crest that looks down over the rocks in the valley. I would really like to know the time detective. Is it 2:30 yet?"

Shaw forces himself not to reply with some smartass answer, gesturing for the man to continue. There's something familiar about the time 2:30, but his memory is struggling to locate the significance.

"But he wasn't scared of heights, either," Edgar says.

"Stop stalling.

"Fear is a funny thing, detective. Everyone is afraid of something. But of all the different things people are afraid of, their reactions are the same. Racing heartbeats, wide eyes, sweating, begging, pleading . . . it's delicious. See, I'm a detective, just like you, only instead of chasing down criminals, I'm searching for fear."

"And the kid?"

"Ah, now he's a brave one. When I told him his family was dead and he was all alone in the world, he didn't show his fear. When I took him into the depths of the mine and threatened to leave him there all alone in the dark, he wasn't afraid. On top of the cliff, looking down at the long drop to the rocks below, he still wasn't scared. But I managed to find his fear. In the end I always manage to discover what it is that someone's truly afraid of."

"What was the boy's fear?"

"The boy, it turns out, is terrified of drowning. Or he was, at least. What time is it, detective?"

Realization rushes through Shaw's neurons like a surging flood. The city's water control structure regulates every day at 2:30 in the afternoon.

"Have they released the pressure on the valves yet today?" Edgar calls after Shaw as he bolts from the room. Racing past the uniform in the hall, he pulls his cell out of his trouser pocket and dials.

"It's Shaw. I need a rescue unit and dive team sent over to the Geede's Water Control Dam by the Green River reservoir. No exact location, but start with the overflow side, near the external ports. I'll meet them there."

Detective Shaw races through the front doors of the precinct, Frank in his uniform close on his heels. He trots across the lot and climbs up into his Jeep. A second door slamming shut echoes his own.

"What the hell are you doing?" he asks Frank, who is donning the passenger seatbelt. "Never mind, there's no time to argue."

Shaw starts the engine, driving the car like a little boy's life depends on it. "Make yourself useful and call the city water works. Get in touch with the engineer in control of maintaining the water pressure and see if it isn't too late to stop him from flicking the switch, will you?"

Reaching out the window, he slaps the magnetic police strobe to his roof and flicks the switch, siren and lights going full force. He does his best to focus on driving, to ignore the conversation taking place in the passenger seat. If the flood gates have been released, he doesn't want to know, doesn't want to chance losing hope and slowing down.

He's made up his mind that he'll be bringing that little boy home alive and he isn't going to fail. He can't fail. Only, that little boy doesn't have a family to come home to anymore. Shaw pushes the

13

thought from his mind and directs his focus on the road.

Frank tries to give him an update, but he waves it away, hitting the rough dirt road that leads to the dam with a jolt that takes years off the life of the Jeep's suspension. Dust billows into the air in an angry cloud around the speeding SUV. Frank clutches at the seatbelt stretched across his chest, willing it to do its job.

Pulling up to the water's edge, Shaw hops out, leaving the Jeep running. He knows the valves have been released by the level of the still rising water. Running over, his pace slows as he enters the maelstrom, struggling against the current. He keeps as close to the structure as he can, searching for any signs of the child.

The sound of rushing water fills his ears like radio static. He loses his footing and stumbles. His head dips beneath the surface of the water, a quick dunk, but in that moment his brain registers what his eyes don't.

Shaw dives back down, using his legs to push himself closer to the wall. His eyes protest against the exposure, but he fights to keep them open, searching for what he knows is there.

His hands find the small recess first. He contorts himself, wrenching his back as he raises his face into the gap of air remaining at the top. He takes a gulp, wraps one arm through a hole in the cinderblock, another around the kid, and propels towards the surface.

The water rushes around them in a frenzy, fighting to wrest the child from his grasp, unwilling to relinquish the prize it had been promised. Shaw labors towards the shore, Frank wading into the turbulent current to help, taking the cinderblock from him. The weight is on such a short length of chain from the boy that the two men almost have to hug as they fight their way back to the sandy bank of the reservoir.

Shaw sets the boy down on the grass and then runs to his Jeep to grab a blanket. He strips the boy's wet shirt off, wrapping the fleece tightly around him. Collapsing on the ground beside the kid, Shaw sits, panting, trying to catch his breath. He pulls his phone out of his pocket and tries to power it on, but that is one battle the water has won.

"Want me to radio it in?" Frank asks.

Still breathless, Shaw gives Frank a thumbs up and waves him to the car. Turning to the boy, he wipes a lock of wet hair as gently as he can from the kid's forehead. The boy stares up at him with huge eyes.

"You're going to be ok, kid," Shaw whispers.

The kid whimpers and then lunges at Shaw, burying his face in the man's chest with such force that he pulls the cinderblock with him. Shaw grunts as he absorbs the impact. Hesitantly, he puts a hand on the kid's back in what he hopes is a gesture of comfort.

He allows himself to relax only when he hears sirens in the distance, heralding the approach of the rescue unit and the end of a long day. The kid in his arms is going to have a hard time, but at least he has the chance. Shaw knows that knowledge is how he is going to live with the memories of what he had seen earlier.

"Where's Jimmy and Allan?" a small voice says from his arms.

"Who are they?" Shaw asks.

"They were with me at my birthday party, when the bad man came."

*****

Back at the station, staring hungrily at the sticky mug rings on the table, Edgar mutters softly to himself, "And you, detective. Did you really think I'd let you off that easily? That I wouldn't discover your fear? In the end I always manage to make my playmates face what it is that they're truly afraid of."

Detecting Fear first appeared in the June 2014 issue of *Suspense Magazine*

It's All About the Cat

It's clear that the cat is a narcissist. Detective Shaw watches the cat stare at its own reflection in the window, licking itself with long, self-indulgent strokes of the tongue. On the floor beneath the window ledge where the cat preens, a woman lays dead in a pool of her own blood. Tiny red paw prints cover the floor. One could almost fool themselves into thinking the cat had been distraught over the woman's death. The missing flesh from the tip of her nose and the way the cat cavalierly ignores all the humans in the room, suggests otherwise.

"Bet you wish he could talk, don't you?" a uniformed officer says, nudging the detective with his elbow.

"He?"

"It's kind of hard not to notice."

Detective Shaw turns toward the uniform, nose wrinkled in distaste.

Mistaking Shaw's reaction, he says, "You must be a dog person."

"Bird, actually."

"Oh! You're the one with the parrot. I've heard about him. The Professor."

"Gilligan."

"I'm Sam."

"The parrot. His name is Gilligan."

"Oh, right. I suppose that makes more sense."

Detective Shaw nods as the crime scene technician gathers her samples and flashes him a thumbs up. He squats next to the corpse, his eyes inspecting the body from head to toe.

"So, if it was you lying here, Gilligan would tell us what happened and who did it, right?"

Shaw squints over his shoulder like an annoying gnat is buzzing in his ear.

"Hey, Petie? This guy's the detective that has the parrot."

"No kidding? I've heard about him. Skipper, right?"

"No, Gilligan."

"Not that, I know the bird's name, dummy. I meant him. Detective Skipper, right?"

Shaw sighs. Standing, he claps his hands together and says, "I'd like to thank everyone for your help, but now it's time to clear the scene."

"What about Percival?"

"Who?" Shaw spins to face the cop called Petie.

"Percival? The cat."

"Oh. If you want to wait around until we're done here, you can take him with you until we notify next of kin if you want."

"Really? Thanks, Detective Skipper."

Shaw closes his eyes, counting until he hears the door shut. When he opens them, he finds the crime scene tech, Shirley, regarding him with sympathy as she tries not to laugh.

"Have you processed the cat yet?"

"Nope. Want to pin him down for me?"

Shaw glances at the cat. Percival yawns, his cat mouth opening impossibly wide, the gaping maw lined with tiny, razored fangs.

"I'll pass."

"Oh, come on. You two are going to have to become friends. You might as well get it over with now."

"What do you mean?"

They stand staring at the cat. Reaching a hand up to his shoulder, Shirley gives it a squeeze. She looks up at him from the corner of her eyes, and says, "It's not just the nose. Look at the left hand."

Shaw follows her suggestion, his gaze zeroing in on the left hand, tucked tight against the body. His pulse quickens as he registers the bone protruding from the bloody stump of the ring finger.

"There's no telling what he may have eaten. That cat is evidence. He's going home with you tonight."

"The hell. Why can't you take him?"

"Can't. Husband's allergic."

"Well, then your husband can stay with me."

Shirley laughs, gives him a grin, then says, "Bet you wish you had a partner right about now, huh?" Shouldering her collection kit, she gathers her evidence bags.

"Where are you going?"

"I've got to get these samples to the lab to process."

"But what about the cat?"

"I lied. I processed him while the M.E. was clearing the body."

"But, wait. You can't leave."

"I'll tell you what. I'll break the bad news to poor Petie. Now, you gentlemen have a good night together, alright?"

He can hear her laughing long after the door shuts behind her.

*****

"I'm sorry."

Another seed pelts the back of his head.

"I said, I'm sorry."

A corn kernel grazes his ear as it zooms by.

"Gilligan."

Feathers rustle as he turns to face the parrot.

"I've locked him in the bathroom, what more do you want from me?"

The bird rolls its pale eyes at him.

"You want to join him?"

Gilligan's head cocks to the side. He shuffles on his perch, turning his back on Shaw.

"Like I don't have enough on my plate."

Detective Shaw returns to his notes, trying to recover his train of thought. The victim was a single white female, early forties, worked as a CPA for one of the larger local accounting firms. According to her neighbors she was quiet, kept to herself. No one could remember her ever having any visitors over. She lived in the coveted top floor apartment in a building with narrow halls and narrower walls, so their assessment on that front was probably accurate.

Her coworkers, who had reported her missing, considered her a hard worker, thorough, dependable, but couldn't remember her ever mentioning any family, friends, or significant other.

The apartment had been beyond neat; every item had its place; every place was a neatly labeled container of some sort. Nothing appeared to have been taken. She didn't own a car. She had no debts or vices that he could detect. As far as he could tell, the victim and her life had been completely unremarkable save for the fact that she had bought the apartment building before moving in, and that she was murdered.

A scratching against the bathroom door is immediately followed by an angry shriek from Gilligan. Shaw walks to the bathroom and cracks the door open. Percival sits staring up at him, fluffy tail curled neatly around his paws. If Shaw didn't know better, he'd say the cat was smirking. Opening the door a little wider, he sees the shredded roll of toilet paper, a puddle of yellow using the grout between the tiles as a flood channel, and a pile of brown on his bathmat.

He shuts the door with a sigh. How could he have forgotten the litter box? Grabbing a wad of paper towels from the kitchen, he wonders how such a small creature could hold so much mess, then freezes as he's struck by another thought. He hadn't brought any food or the cat's water dish, either.

Sinking down onto one of the kitchen chairs, he goes over the apartment in his mind, mentally revisiting each room. For the life of him, he can't recall seeing any of the accoutrements that one would expect to accompany cat ownership. Even his own place bore traces of Gilligan in every room, and the parrot spent most of his time in a cage, albeit with an open door.

Rummaging through his cupboards, Detective Shaw finds an out of date can of tuna, which he dumps onto a paper plate. Filling a bowl with water, he presents both to the cat, hoping to not incur any additional wrath. Bagging the evidence, he shoves the bathmat in a trash bag and gives the floor a quick cleaning before returning to his desk.

*****

Shaw arrives at the station early the next morning, and he's already made two stops. The first was the apartment building of his crime scene, where he had hung a poster displaying the very best of his limited arts and crafts skills. The second was a pet store, where he spent a ridiculous amount of money purchasing cat food and a litter box, and though he'd never admit it, a cat bed and a few toys.

After leaving several baggies of 'evidence' on Shirley's desk, he heads over to the Medical Examiner's Office to check on his victim. Entering the autopsy suite, he finds Doc Hastings working over the deceased on the examination table.

"Morning, Doc."

"Detective Shaw! Heard you have yourself a new roommate."

"Don't people have anything better to talk about?"

"Good news travels fast."

"I think your definition of good differs from mine."

Hastings smirks.

"Do you have anything that would help with, oh, I don't know, the case?"

"You're no fun today."

"I'm no fun every day."

"True." Returning his attention to the body, Hastings says. "The findings on your victim are pretty cut and dried. She suffered from a single stab wound to the chest. The left ventricle was severed. It's likely she was immediately incapacitated. Would have been unconscious as she bled out."

"What can you tell me about the weapon."

"I took a cast of the wound for you, but I feel fairly confident that you're looking for a pair of scissors."

"Really? You ever work a case where scissors were used in a pre-mediated act?"

"I've actually never worked one where scissors were used in a murder. I had one where a lady was running and tripped and stabbed herself once."

"That actually happens?"

"Apparently."

"Hmm. Any defensive wounds?"

"Not even a scratch. Poor gal never saw it coming."

"That's consistent with the theory I'm working."

"Care to share?"

"Not really."

"Ouch. At least tell me about the decedent. Who was she? The cranky spinster? A crazy cat lady?"

"I don't think either would really apply."

"But she had a cat."

"Maybe. Maybe not."

Placing the victim's liver on the scale, Hastings speaks the weight into his Dictaphone, giving Shaw a dirty look over the top of his glasses. "Why are you being so difficult today? Are you missing the cat?"

"What?"

"Nothing. So, we're thinking it wasn't premeditated. Do you concur?" Hastings asks.

"I do."

"Which means it was either a crime of opportunity or passion."

"There are other options," Shaw says.

"Such as?"

"An accident."

"Is that what you think this was?"

"No, not entirely."

"Are you trying to crush my last nerve?"

"I am not."

"Then say something useful. Or interesting. Either will do." Hastings dictates the weight and appearance of the kidneys, then peers at Shaw over his glasses once more. "You may begin."

Crossing his arms, Shaw leans against the empty dissection table behind him, the metal cold through the thin fabric of his slacks. "We agree that the crime was not planned."

"Correct."

"And the victim doesn't have any defensive wounds, which would support that she didn't see the attack coming."

"Tell me something I don't know."

"The cat belongs to the killer."

"Wait. What?" Hastings stops, arms frozen in the act of running the bowel.

"There were no signs that the cat belonged in the apartment. No water dish, no food, no cat box. Nothing."

"Now, that is interesting."

Shaw nods. "I think the cat belongs to one of the other tenants in the building. I think the cat followed his owner upstairs when they went to talk to the victim and got left behind when the killer panicked after committing the crime."

"So, what are the other tenants in the building like?"

"They're all women."

"Ah, so it's the killer who's the crazy cat lady, not the victim. What are you thinking for motive?"

"I haven't a clue."

"Then, for your sake, Detective, I hope your theory pans out."

Detective Shaw's phone sounds the Jaws theme from his coat pocket. He glances at the screen, then heads towards the door. "With any luck, this'll be my proof."

Shaw waits for the doors to swing shut behind him before answering.

"Hello."

"Um, yes, I think you found my cat."

The voice on the other end of the line is that of an older female. He quickly matches it to one of the faces he saw while interviewing the neighbors the day before.

"I just may have. Can you describe the cat for me?"

An irritated sigh is followed by a beat of silence. "Really."

"Well . . ."

"If you insist. He's a Siamese, blue eyes, tan and chocolate fur, has a collar with the name Percival on it."

"Yep, that's the cat I found."

"When can you return him?"

"When would be convenient for you?"

Another sigh, like he's being difficult. "I'd like him returned as soon as possible."

"Well, I'm at work, but if I left now, I could pick the cat up and be there within an hour if that would work for you?"

"I suppose it'll have to, won't it?"

"And what's the address?"

"What kind of question is that? You put the flyer up, don't you remember?"

"I put flyers up in several buildings in the area, ma'am," Shaw lied. "I found the cat out by my trash cans. I wasn't sure which building the cat may have come from."

"My Percival never would have gone outside on his own. There's no reward, you know."

"I'm not interested in a reward, ma'am, I just want to return the cat to his rightful owner."

"Hmf. Well, it took you long enough. He's been gone almost three days already."

"The address, ma'am?"

"82 Elm, #3. I'll expect you within the hour."

Pocketing the phone, Shaw pokes his head back into the autopsy suite and asks, "Hey, Doc. You got a time of death for me, yet?"

"Myofilament decomposition would place death between 60 to 75 hours."

"Perfect, Doc, thanks. Gotta run."

"Yeah, yeah. You detectives are all the same. You only want me for my . . ." Finding himself alone, Doc Hastings sighs, returning his attention to the task at hand.

*****

The door opens, revealing a sturdy looking woman in her sixties, a scowl below her glasses, frown lines in heavily creased folds above them.

"Where's my cat?"

Shaw flashes his badge. "I'm Detective Shaw, ma'am. We spoke yesterday about your neighbor." He gestures with his eyes to the apartment above them.

"I told you everything I have to say. I'm busy."

"Waiting for Percival?"

Her face scrunches, eyes narrowed, lips puckered. "What do you know about that?"

"You called me earlier. I made the flyer." Hearing a snicker from further down the hallway, Shaw clears his throat loudly. "I'm the one who found your cat."

"Percival would never leave the building. He never goes anywhere without me. I've had him since he was a kitten. He follows me around like a puppy dog."

"That's just what I suspected."

"It is?"

"Yes. Which is why I have this warrant here granting me permission to search your apartment."

She snatches the paper from his outstretched hand, glaring at him as she skims the text.

"This is ridiculous. You're not coming in. You're not welcomed."

Footsteps approach as Shaw says, "That piece of paper says I don't need a welcome. Now, if you'll step aside, ma'am."

"I most certainly will not!"

Two uniformed officers step up, one at each of Shaw's elbows.

"You don't understand," she says. Her body deflates as Shaw squeezes past her into the apartment.

"I understand enough," Shaw says. "I understand that your cat, the one that follows you around like a dog, was found in the victim's apartment upstairs. I understand that you've already put a call in to the property management company, requesting to move to the victim's apartment. And," Shaw says, pointing to a sheet of paper on the kitchen counter, "I understand that you have a piece of the victim's mail in your possession. Ask Shirley to bag this, will you, boys?"

"You don't understand," she repeats. "Look at that bill," she gestures to the piece of stolen mail on the counter. "Look at what she pays. $60 in the middle of winter in Massachusetts. $60! Do you know what I pay? Closer to $200! I can't keep paying that on my pension. What was I supposed to do? Keep letting her steal all my heat for free after she stole my apartment?"

Shaw lifts an eyebrow.

"My ability to get by on my retirement was based on living in that apartment with that heating bill. I started out on the ground floor of this place almost twenty years ago and have been working my way up since. When the last tenant was moved to a care home, somehow that witch swooped in and stole the apartment from me. Then, when I went up there to ask her to split the electric bill since I was paying for her heat, she refused. Threatened to have me evicted for stealing her mail."

"Got it!" Shirley came out of the bathroom, a pair of scissors held up triumphantly in one of her gloved hands. In the other, she held a cotton swab with a pink tip.

"I didn't mean to . . . I didn't mean what happened. Honest. I was just so mad. When she refused to tell me how she finagled her way into the apartment that was rightfully mine . . ."

"I've got the answer to that one," Shaw says. "She actually had every right to the apartment."

He watches her face turn several shades of purple.

"You see, she bought the building." Without waiting for a response, Shaw gives the uniformed officers a nod and leaves, the click of the handcuffs following him out the door.

*****

Detective Shaw struggles to unlock the door, maintaining a precarious grip on the bags he's juggling. "Gilligan, I'm home." Shaw sets the bags on the table, untwisting the noose one of the plastic handles has dug into his wrist. "Gilligan?"

Entering the living room, the first thing he sees is the open bathroom door. The second is the empty birdcage.

"Gilligan!"

A halfhearted squawk carries from the couch. Shaw stares at the scene, sinking slowly into the armchair behind him. The cat opens his blue eyes just a slit and smirks at him, then stretches his back legs farther across the couch. Behind him, the parrot continues to groom the fur behind the cat's ear with his beak. Pausing, he cocks his head at Shaw, whistles, and says, "Pretty kitty."

"Don't be an enabler," Shaw says. Covering his face with his hand, he can't help peeking through his fingers. He grins.

It's All About The Cat was first featured by *The Saturday Evening Post* in March of 2019

Dying Print

She burst through the door in a perfumed whirlwind of fear. Pausing just inside the entrance, her nervous gaze roams over the patrons of the diner. I feel it pass over me as I focus on the plate of runny eggs I'm eating. A rush of heat flares up under my collar as her stare settles on me with laser beam intensity. It's no surprise when I find myself in her shadow a moment later as she stands over me in the booth where I sit.

I busy myself with chewing a slice of bacon. When it becomes apparent she isn't going to let me ignore her, I look up, straight into her desperate eyes. They plead with me from the clear skin of her unlined face, high cheekbones chiseled from alabaster, her full lips pulled into a tight line. Her dress is old-fashioned, like something women wore in the fifties. Collar buttoned at a modest depth, fitted waist, loose skirt that falls just below the knees.

She is beautiful. They always are, though, the ones in trouble. As I wait for her to speak, I recall the first lesson I learned about beautiful women, years ago during a slice of summer spent with my grandparents, an overheard passing of wisdom from my grandmother to my sister. 'You're a lovely girl, Faye, you're going to be a beautiful woman, so you're going to have to be careful and make wise decisions. Beautiful women attract trouble like a magnet.'

Her lips part. I lay my fork down in anticipation of her words.

"Are you a cop?"

"Is it that obvious?" I ask, directing a pointed look at the two uniformed officers sitting at the counter enjoying an uninterrupted slice of pie with their coffee. Why me?

"I need help." She slides uninvited onto the booth bench across from me. When I don't comment, she continues, glancing around suspiciously. "Someone is after me."

"Have you filed a report?"

"I have." That surprises me. Reaching into her purse, she retrieves a folded piece of paper. She has both hands placed over it, guarding it. "I'm not sure they're taking it seriously."

"Do you know who is after you?"

She shakes her head no. She starts to speak, stops herself, and then sighs deeply. "I, uh, upset a lot of people in my line of work. I'm an editor for a large magazine. I get a lot of hate mail from upset writers."

"What makes this time any different?"

"Well, the letter came to my home address, which was a first. And when I went to my car a few minutes ago, I discovered that someone had broken in and left a little present behind."

Pushing my plate of cold slop to the side, I lean forward, prompting her to continue with a raise of my eyebrows.

"There's, I don't know, a figure hanging from the rearview mirror, kind of made me think of a voodoo doll. It's been stabbed through with a pen."

My interest is piqued. "Detective Shaw." I extend my hand. She accepts the invitation, her small, pale hand losing itself in mine.

"Shelly Piper," she says.

*****

As I pay the bill and follow Shelly to her car, I think about the second lesson I learned about beautiful women, this wisdom gleaned from my own powers of observation. Beautiful women are either shrinkers or growlers. When confronted with the trouble that inevitably comes their way, they either shrink or growl.

A sleaze ball in a grocery store, a group of hoodlums on the street, whenever I see it coming, I always find something to feign interest in while I wait to see what happens. Will the woman shrink, panicked eyes desperately searching for someone to step in and rescue her? Or will she growl, refusing to back down to her would be antagonist, showing no signs of fear or weakness. Unfortunately, there's no difference in the statistics of which type falls victim to violent crime more often.

I wonder which type Shelly is. Watching the way she strides right over to her car, throws the door open and points at the offending intruder, I'm guessing a growler. This means she must be pretty scared if she's making herself vulnerable enough to ask for help.

Ducking my head into the car, I'm enveloped in the warm aroma of vanilla. I take a deep breath, resisting the urge to shut my eyes and lose myself in the happy kitchen memories from my youth that surface whenever I'm exposed to the scent. Instead, I inspect the talisman that's looped around the mirror, swaying gently in the fall breeze that enters through the open door. There's nothing warm or fuzzy about it.

The dangling dolly appears handmade. It's actually quite skillfully crafted; a very good replica of its intended idol. Someone spent a lot of time on it.

The skin appears to be made from soft, pale leather. The features, achieved with delicate stitches of colored thread, most definitely resemble Shelly's. The hair is the same cut and shade, and I have a feeling that, should I get close enough, it would have the same sweet smell of apples wafting from it. The dress it wears is quite like the one Shelly has on now, the pattern a dark grey houndstooth print against lighter grey wool. A red pen has been stabbed through the heart of the doll.

"That." Shelly points with a shaking hand, her wrist so close to me that I hear the soft jangle of her bracelets knocking together with the tremors. "What it's wearing is made from a dress that went missing from the laundry room at my apartment building. Whoever did this not only know where I live, they've been there. They've been close enough to me to see me wash my laundry."

I retreat from the car and face her. "Miss Piper."

"Shelly."

I nod. "Shelly. I'm going to call a crime scene tech out here to see what they can find. We'll take this little present here to the lab and analyze every stitch until we have something that will help us find out who your fan is. I don't think it's anything to worry about, but I will take this investigation seriously and treat this as a valid threat. That work for you?"

"Fair enough."

*****

I take her back inside the diner and order us a round of coffee even though her knee jitters up and down like a piston on high test as she sits across from me. I've chosen a table by the door, so I can watch for the tech's truck. The coffee comes, the waitress sloshing half of it into the saucer as she sets it down.

I move my mug closer, so I can breathe the rising steam. Shelly's staring over my head, and I realize she's watching the door. Taking my pen and notepad from my pocket, I draw her attention. She gives me a tired smile.

"So. When did you file the report?"

"Yesterday."

"Is that when the letter came to your house?"

"Yes."

"And that's why you filed the report? Because the letter was delivered to your home address?"

"Yes. Why else would I have taken it so seriously?"

"That's right. You say that you get a lot of angry letters."

"I do."

"And this is because of your job as an editor, you said?"

"Yes, that's correct."

"But other than the place of delivery, there was nothing different about this letter?"

"I don't think so. No."

"Was there anything in the content of the letter that was different from the other hate mail you get? More threats or violence? A different tone? Anything that makes you associate it as being by someone who's written you this sort of thing before?"

"I don't understand."

"As an editor I'm sure you pick up on things as you read. A peculiar style of syntax? Notable diction, maybe?"

She shakes her head, and I notice a hardness about the set of her jaw, like I'm irritating her. She pushes her hair behind her ear and exhales a noisy puff of air from her nose. I suddenly get the impression that I'm keeping her from more important things, when a flash draws my attention through the window. The white crime scene pick-up is bouncing across the rutted parking lot, light from the diner shining off the reflective paint on the Site Commander camper covering the bed.

Rising from the table, I can see the red and white news van that has followed the truck into the lot. The bottom feeding vultures on B-roll duty have arrived.

"Is that a news crew?" Shelly asks.

"Yeah. You can stay here. I'll deal with of them."

My hand is sticky from where I touched the table to get up. I fight the urge to wipe it on my pants. While I look for a more appropriate cleaner, Shelly pops out of her chair like a jack-in-the-box. I see her check her reflection in the window before she bolts outside.

I curse, chasing after her while I run my gooey hand over the side of my slacks. She bypasses the forensic tech and heads straight for the news van. The bored twenty-something in the passenger seat takes notice, his eyes widening as she nears him. I see her damsel in distress act, part two, play out and I feel a twinge in my gut, almost like jealousy. I move in front of Shelly as the kid hops out of the van, pulling his coat on as he barks at the camera man to hurry up.

"Shelly, this isn't a good idea."

"Whoever it is needs to know I'm not afraid." Throwing her shoulders back, lower lip jutting out, she returns my disapproving look. A flame sparks in her eyes. Defiance? Or something else?

"There are better ways." I tell her. "Antagonizing a possible obsessive stalker type could make the situation escalate. This isn't the way to handle it."

"Am I breaking the law?"

"No but . . ." I'm left shaking my head as she steps around me to talk with the news anchor.

"Looks like trouble to me." Lou, the forensic tech, is leaning against the back of his truck, a sardonic smile dripping off his face. I suspect there's a wink somewhere within the folds of his weathered skin, but I don't see it. I'm hoping to be treated kinder by gravity than poor Lou.

I give him a synopsis of what's going on and watch him go to work like a blood hound, both in action and appearance. Standing to the side, I divide my attention between him and Shelly. Shelly gets more. I watch her play to the camera as she's interviewed, can hear her strong, brave, yet worried voice floating through the air. I tune in for snippets.

"Yes, I'm an editor at Mystery Madness magazine. And I definitely think that this is the act of a disgruntled writer . . . we try to be fair, but we can't publish everything, we have a standard to maintain, but to violate my personal space, to make such threats . . . well, of course I'm frightened. Wouldn't you be?"

Lou finishes as the interview wraps up. He has the mutilated doll in a plastic evidence bag and has lifted hair, fibers and prints from the vehicle. He asks Shelly if he can take her prints for comparison. She avoids my gaze as he pushes her fingers down into the inkpad and rolls each finger firmly on the paper. Then he closes all the compartments on the camper and drives off, leaving us alone.

Shelly stares at her car as she works to clean her fingertips with a towelette Lou gave her.

"He pressed down really hard. It kind of hurt."

"Most people say that. They've got to roll the finger firmly to get an impression of the ridges."

"So, that's just how they take prints then? He wasn't mad at me?"

Her lips pout into a small smile and I get the impression she's asking about me. I shake my head. "I guess we're done here. You'll be okay driving home?"

She nods and pulls her keys out of a tiny purse. She stands with her hand on the door. I can see the gears turning in her head but can't translate what they're working towards.

"Is there anything else I can help you with?"

She waits too long before she says no. I pretend not to notice.

"I'll keep in touch, then. Let you know if we turn anything up at the lab."

I pull the car door open for her. She moves to get in, then stops. "Thank you, detective." She slides behind the wheel.

I force a small smile, close the car door, and walk away. I consider going back into the diner, ordering another meal, but decide against it. I know I should go home and get some sleep, but I know that isn't happening either, so I head to the station. For some reason I have this insatiable itch to look at the letter Shelly got.

*****

I get waylaid on my way to the station by a BOLO for a kid who held up a convenience store. Described as over six feet tall with curly red hair, wearing red high-tops and a yellow windbreaker, I was debating whether to radio in a comment about his known accomplice, the Hamburglar, when I see Ronald McDonald himself walking down the street.

The kid was a quick collar. By the time a uniform swung by to pick him up, the shift leader had made the scene and ordered me home. Once there, two fingers of Dewar's and I was off to a restless sleep haunted by dolls with sewn x eyes, a stitched line mouth and shapely human legs protruding from beneath a stiff paper skirt.

I'm driving in the next morning, two jumbo cups of the gas station's best coffee in the cup holder beside me, when I get the call. Dispatch radios me the address, I hit my lights and siren, and race across town to Shelly's apartment. I pull up in front of the three-story brownstone and double park on the street.

Shelly opens the door before I can knock, greeting me in a mid-calf pink bathrobe. She invites me in and takes a seat at the kitchen table, drawing her legs up under the robe. Dark red toenails peak out, a stark contrast to her pale skin – and to how I had perceived her personality. I guess I had expected she was more of a pale pink girl, something understated, demure.

I lean against the wall, just inside the door, waiting. She stares at her toes a long minute before meeting my eyes. The fingers of her right hand pull nervously at her lip. Finally, she gestures with her free hand. I followed the direction of her outstretched arm to a length of kitchen counter. A porcelain bowl painted with purple flowers sits on the corner.

"I always throw my car keys in there," Shelly says.

Peering into the bowl, I see the note, red markered words glaring angrily up at me. 'Be glad I didn't take you, too.'

"And your car?" I ask.

"Gone."

"I'm gonna call a tech out, see if we can't find any prints or trace. And a uniform to take your statement for the report. Until then, try not to walk between the counter and the door, we might be able to get some shoe prints with an electrostatic lifter. Shelly?"

I have a feeling she hasn't heard a word I've said. She's staring vacantly at the wall, still playing with her lip. "Shelly?"

"Someone was in my house." She says it slowly, like I don't already know. "While I was sleeping."

"I understand you're upset . . ."

"Do you?" She looks up at me and for the first time I see a trace of something hard in her eyes. It makes her look dangerous.

"I can help you get the locks changed if you want. And I can see about having a patrol keep an eye on you while we're working this out."

She gives an amused huff, the air pushing nosily out of her nose. "That won't be necessary."

"I really think . . ."

"No, it's ok. I'll take care of it. Why don't you just call your people to do what they need to do so I can get to work?"

I'm a little taken back by the sharpness of her tone, her attitude, but it's nothing I'm not used to. "Sure," I say, all business. "Whatever I can do to make this easier on you, ma'am. It would be helpful if you made a list of people who might have a grudge against you. Maybe some of the writers you've rejected recently?"

"I started on it last night, actually." She stands, gliding out of the kitchen and into the living room. She settles onto the couch, pulls the laptop off the glass coffee table onto her legs, and opens it.

"Would it be possible for you to print me a copy?"

She gives no indication of hearing me. A moment later I hear a sheet of paper being sucked into a printer, ink spitting out into a list of names. Pushing the laptop back onto the table, she stands with an air of annoyance and walks to the hallway. Pulling open a folding door, she grabs the paper from the printer tray on the shelf over the washing machine and thrusts it at me. Thanking her for her assistance, I back out of the room, placing the call from the warmth of the unheated hallway.

*****

After a stop for more coffee, I'm on my way to the station, again, when I'm stopped. Again. I plug the address dispatch gives me into my GPS and travel down the roads at maddening speed. I'm too late.

Pulling up, a circus of mayhem unfolds before me. I drag myself out of the car and am instantly spotted by the spider eyes of the two news crews already at the scene. I put a hand up to ward off their attack, quickening my step to reach the taped boundary of the crime scene before they can cut off my path.

"What've we got?" I ask the nearest uniform I can find. He rocks on his heels, thumbs hooked in his belt loops. Turning his buzzed cut head toward me, he moves the toothpick he's sucking on to the corner of his mouth and speaks. "Car in the water."

I can plainly see the car being hauled out of the water by a tow truck. I open my mouth to speak again but close it upon catching a glimpse of my reflection in his Ray Bans. Or rather, the reflection of what is approaching behind me. I spin around to face her, cursing under my breath.

"Is it mine?" Shelly shouts, one hand pushing the tape up as she ducks to move under.

"Whoa, ma'am, I've gotta ask you to stop right there," Ray Bans says, rushing over to prevent her from crossing the line.

I take my time approaching. "I don't know, Shelly, I just got here. You must've got word right after I did. Mind if I ask how?"

"It's not important. All I want to know is if that's my car? Did some pathetic pyscho really dump my car in the lake?"

By now the news crews have swarmed like blow flies to a bloated corpse in summer. Shelly turns to face them, all wide eyes and distressed damsel. I watch for a few seconds as she plays up to them, telling her story, poor editor being stalked by a disgruntled writer, then I use the show Shelly is putting on as an opportunity to slip away undetected.

The car has just been pulled onto land, streams of scummy water pouring off in torrents as the tow truck driver hauls it up the embankment and parks. It's a four-door sedan, maroon, and I know it's the same car I was in last night even before I match the VIN to the one registered to Shelly's plates. Maybe it's the handmade, Voodoo-like doll in the driver's seat, a larger version of last night's, that gave it away. The press is going to love it. It'll be like a classroom of kids on candy the last day before Christmas break.

The buzzards strain to get a better view of what's going on, cameras panning between the car and Shelly. I can see the crime scene truck and a pair of marked police vehicles approaching. I prepare for the distraction, ready to make a hasty exit as soon as the moment strikes. Two minutes later I'm in my car, heading for the station. This time I'm determined to make it.

*****

Once at the precinct I pull the file from Shelly's initial complaint and carry it to my desk with a tall cup of coffee and a stack of papers from my car. Taking a sip from the steaming mug, I open the folder, skimming the report before flipping to the offending letter, sheathed in a plastic casing. There is no evidence report on it. It has not been sent to trace, never been checked for prints. Like most threatening letters that are brought to us it has simply been stuck into a clear holder that would preserve it and filed away.

The tone of the letter is hostile, but no particular threats are made. There's also not a reference to the specific offense that Shelly committed to gain her admirer's attention. All in all, it strikes me as generic and benign. Based on the evidence before me, I never would have guessed that the perp behind the letter would have escalated to a more active role.

A squiggle in the lower right corner gets me excited. I think there's a fiber, maybe some trace for the lab to analyze, but on closer inspection I realize it's an ink mark from the printer. It could still prove useful. I shuffle through the stack of papers from my car, looking for the list of possible suspects Shelly gave me, trying not to get my hopes up while contemplating the degree of difficulty in getting a printer sample from every name on the list for comparison.

"Hey, Shaw." Turk Johnson, the vice detective who sits at the desk behind me calls my name at the same time he bounces a wadded sheet of paper off the back of my head. I catch the projectile before it can hit the floor. Spinning in my chair, I shoot it back at him.

"Yeah, Turk?"

"This you?"

He spins the monitor enough so I can see the screen, but I get up anyway and walk around his desk, standing beside him to watch. It's news footage from the car scene I've just left. In the upper left corner, above Shelly's shoulder, I watch myself peer into the interior of the vehicle and then say a few words to the officer on scene before disappearing.

"I thought you always managed to avoid the circus," Turk says.

Something about the look on Shelly's face strikes me in a way I can't yet identify but need to determine. Ignoring Turk's comment, I ask, "Can you play it again? This time with sound?"

"Sure thing."

I absorb every move, look, and gesture Shelly makes. Every word she says is perfect, no stumbling or hesitation. Her confidence, the way she directs the interview, stealing the show from the news anchor, leading him down the road she wants to go amazes even me. It's like . . .

"Nothing like free publicity, huh?" Turk asks.

Nodding silently, I return to my desk. Turk is right. Shelly is definitely making the most of the situation, spinning it to her advantage. She's made it to A feed, a headline story. Everyone watching now knows which magazine she is the editor of and that it is a periodical of discerning taste that prints only the best stories.

I find myself unable to tune my attention back to the task at handle, my brain struggling to make a connection I sense but am not yet wholly aware of. When I pick up Shelly's list, the synapses in my brain finally wake up and fire, zinging me with the answer like a snap from a rubber band.

*****

Shelly sits across the table from me, an irritated look on her face. Maybe she feels like I'm wasting her time. Or maybe it's something about this tiny box of a room that reeks of smoker's sweat that doesn't sit well with her. Either way, I take my time, shuffling papers, skimming notes, drawing the process out. Finally, she breaks the uncomfortable silence that fills the room like an elephant's fart.

"Detective Shaw? Why, exactly, am I here? I honestly can't think of anything that I haven't told you already that can help with the investigation."

A knock rattles the door and the district attorney slips inside, nose wrinkling as her senses encounter the room's odor. I rise halfway in my seat the way my grandma and a rolled-up newspaper in her fist taught me to do when a lady enters a room. The DA sinks into the chair next to me, placing a folder on her lap, hands on her grey slacks like she's afraid to touch anything in the room she doesn't have to. I don't blame her.

"Shelly, this is Marjorie Grace, our district attorney. Ms. Grace is here today to discuss your options with you."

"I don't understand." Shelly's eyes flit between me and Ms. Grace, looking for a clue. "What are you going to do, give me a restraining order against the invisible man and we'll just hope he leaves me alone?"

"No." Ms. Grace's chilly tone oozes distain so openly that Shelly flinches as if struck. "Actually, Ms. Piper, I'm here to present you with a cease-and-desist order and to discuss with you your options for making restitution to this department, as well as a possible jail term."

Shelly looks to me as if I can save her. I stare into her damsel in distress eyes, noticing the tiny red lines that crisscross the white like a spider's web. Her chin trembles. Her gaze falls to her lap, her face flushing a deep pink, and I think she is blushing with shame. Then her eyes flash up and focus on mine with such intensity that I can feel the searing heat and I realize it's anger.

"How?" Shelly asks.

"Little things. The same ink print mark on the hate letter and the list you printed out for me. The washer and dryer in your apartment when you said the dress used to make the doll's clothes was stolen from the laundry room of your apartment building, which doesn't exist. The way you showed up to the dump site when we found your car. Your blatant use of the press coverage for free publicity. Take your pick."

I settle back into my chair, crossing my arms. I watch Shelly's trembling grow more violent as she becomes unable to contain her rage. Her hands grasp the metal arms of the chair, nails digging in with such force that they bend under the pressure, breaking. Then, just as quickly as her nails snapped, her entire demeanor changes. She nervously licks her lips, holding her hands out in supplication like she's begging for our help.

"Everybody with their Kindles and iPads and Nooks." She spits the words out like a bad taste. "Nobody wants to hold a paper copy in their hand anymore. My magazine was going under. I couldn't let that happen. A bit of mystery and scandal is healthy for the economy. It's what the people want. The news channels get viewers, my magazine gets readers, and no one gets hurt. Please." She searches both of our faces for a trace of compassion. Finding none, she whispers, "I did what I did out of love for the printed word. Can you really fault me for that?"

Dying Print first appeared in February 2019 issue of *The Wild Musette Journal*

A Little Bit of Murderer

"You're absolutely positive that the door was locked when you got here?" Detective Shaw asked the young, uniformed officer, a look of doubt on his face.

"Yes, sir. We got the landlord to unlock the door for us, but it was dead bolted from the inside. We had to take the door off the hinges to gain entrance."

"What did you touch when you went inside?"

"Nothing, sir. We could tell that the guy was dead from the doorway. We called you and the crime scene techs immediately. I never even stepped a foot across the threshold."

"Hmmm." This case was already causing the detective's gut to sour. "And the windows?"

"Nailed shut, sir. One of the techs tried to open one after dusting for prints. She said she wanted to crack it a little, let some fresh air in. You know, because of the smell."

"There's a smell?" the detective deadpanned. He didn't need some snot nosed kid to explain to him that the room reeked. The tenant must have had ten cats – and no litter box – in the tiny studio apartment. He'd have to check with animal control later, see how many they had removed. Luckily, they hadn't started gnawing on the corpse yet.

"And the room was searched?"

"Yes, sir, when the techs got here, they had my partner secure the scene. Checked the closet, the shower, under the bed . . ."

"And the techs found?"

"Nothing of interest, sir. They did a thorough search, I watched them, but with all this mess . . ."

"Uhuh. And the M.E.?"

"The Medical Examiner said the preliminary indications pointed to strangulation, but the ligature wasn't with the body. It had been removed."

"So. The door was bolted from the inside, the windows were nailed shut, the guy on the bed was dead, but his death was a homicide, so at some point, someone was in here with him, and they had to have gotten out some way."

"That's right, sir. We have ourselves a real locked room mystery. I thought those only happened on TV." The young cop's eyes shone with excitement.

"They do. There's always an explanation. Always." The kid was annoying him, this case was annoying him, and the stench of cat piss was annoying him. He'd had enough. "Well, thanks for your help, officer. I'm sure there are other matters that need your attention. I've got this from here." He gleaned a small bit of joy from the disappointed look earned by his dismissal. He turned his back on the kid to make sure he got his point across, heard the trudge of reluctant steps as the kid shuffled toward the elevator. Now he could get to work.

He started to the right of the door, where the floor met the wall, and followed the union around the room, moving furniture, avoiding cat piles, until he found himself at the door again. A solid hour of scouring produced nothing at the floor seam and nothing in the walls. He grabbed a broom, which had probably never been used, and began exploring where the ceiling met the wall, again traveling around the room. He painstakingly probed every inch of the ceiling with the broom handle. He poked at the junction of the ceiling fan, with its oversized, frond shaped blades. Still nothing.

Changing tactics, he searched the room for a plastic bag that wasn't dripping with cat piss, then used it to protect his slacks as he got down on his hands and knees, methodically trying every tile on the floor. Even after moving the bed, refrigerator, and stove to check under them, he still came up with nothing. He checked under the sink. He checked the window frames. Checked the nails that bound them shut. He checked the glass in the sills. He checked the door frame. He checked the locks and the hinges.

Stepping into the hall for a breather, he called the Medical Examiner's Office. Cause of death had been conclusively determined. The victim was strangled. Trace evidence suggested a cable coated with plastic. Their best guess was an old-fashioned phone cord.

Detective Shaw went back into the room, crossed to where he had encountered the ancient relic of a phone during his search. He confirmed that the cord was missing. So, if the stiff had somehow managed to strangle himself, where had the cord gone to?

He tossed the place, moving the contents from one corner of the room to the other, searching every inch for the missing phone cord, but he couldn't find it anywhere. He even checked the toilet tank, down the drains, inside the oven, the cabinets, and the refrigerator.

He wasn't ready to give up, but he couldn't think of anything else to try. The thought disgusted him, but maybe the kid was right. Maybe this was one of those locked door mysteries they needed Sherlock Holmes to solve. He strung crime scene tape across the door. The scene should be fine for a bit while he went downstairs to get some fresh air and clear his head.

After Detective Shaw had been gone for a few minutes, there was a shuffling sound. Soft grunts uttered with exertion. A thud on the floor. It hadn't been an easy life for Timmy Boyles. He'd never enjoyed being a little person. He couldn't stand the slur midget.

He grunted again as he yanked at the phone cord, trying to free it from the oversized fan blade so far above his head. He held on tight, making sure his bungee didn't snap up, out of his reach. With a final tug, it came down. Coiling it neatly, he put it in his pocket. It wasn't fun being thirty pounds and having your face at knee level. But, he thought as he walked under the crime scene tape and out the door, sometimes it had its perks.

A Little Bit Of Murderer first appeared in the March 2014 issue of *Twisted Endings Magazine*

It's In the Bag

Detective Shaw tapped the toe of his size thirteen boot impatiently. Tired of waiting, he headed down the hall, his steps echoing off the bone colored cinderblock walls. Like most lower-level government institutions, the place was Spartan. And understaffed. Bracing himself, he pushed through the maroon double doors at the end of the hall, entering the autopsy suite.

The fishy smell of old blood assaulted his nose. The buzz of flies competed with the static hum of the florescent lights overhead. The woman working over the body on the metal slab gave a startled shout.

Detective Shaw stopped just inside the door, grabbed a pair of shoe covers from the rack and slipped them on as he apologized. "Sorry, Pam. Didn't mean to sneak up on you like that." He debated whether or not to grab a pair of gloves. Deciding he wouldn't need them, he walked across the drab cement floor, ignoring the random strands of hair and blood splotches that littered its surface.

She stared at him wide eyed, almost guiltily, as if he had caught her red handed. Technically, he had. "I came in through the back. The buzzer sounded. No one came out."

"Sorry about that," Pam said. "Jerry must have left for lunch. I didn't hear it." She went back to stuffing the orange biohazard bag of organs into the body cavity, struggling to get it to fit. "Doctor Hastings has already left for the day. He didn't say you'd be dropping in."

"He didn't know. I was just passing by, decided to stop and see if he'd gotten the lab results back on the John Doe from last week."

He watched as she deftly finished tucking the bag into its confines, replaced the breastplate, and pulled the skin flaps together.

"The floater?"

Shaw nodded.

"Yep, the results are on board four." She gestured with her head towards the rack of clipboards hung next to the door of the walk-in cooler. He crossed over, looked down at his bare hands. Pam, busily sewing the body closed, long curved needle drawing the thin rope through the flesh like she was trussing a turkey, looked up and noticed. "Heroin overdose."

She finished closing the incision and tied off the knot. Placing the needle on the instrument tray, she peeled off her top layer of gloves and tossed them into the biohazard waste container. Walking over, she picked up the board for him, held it so he could read it. Shaw scanned the report quickly, nodding when he was done.

"Thanks."

"Anytime."

"So, how do you like it here so far?"

"It's good. Different. A lot busier than the last Medical Examiner's Office I worked for, but that's a good thing, right? For us at least. And everyone's so nice here."

"Glad to hear it."

The extent of his small talk skills tapped, an awkward silence hung between them.

"Well, I'll tell Dr. Hastings that you stopped by."

"Great." Detective Shaw made a hasty retreat, pausing by the door to ditch his shoe covers. "Thanks for your help."

Pam nodded and waved, watching his retreat until the doors stopped swinging and she was once again by herself in the sanctity of the autopsy suite.

The sun was setting but the heat was still oppressive when Detective Shaw pulled up in front of the apartment building. A patch of scrubby grass fronted the two-story brown brick structure. The call had come over the radio just a few moments before. Usually, a uniformed officer would handle an initial missing person's check, but he'd been only a few streets over, on his way home after a late day, and he needed a distraction from a case that seemed to have hit a dead end.

A distraction like Betsy Mays. The woman's employer had taken the time to drive down to the precinct to file a report. For the last week Ms. Mays had failed to show up to the small office where she worked. All calls, texts, and emails had gone unanswered. Attempts to get in touch with her new roommate had failed as well.

Cases like this usually went one of two ways. Either the person in question simply no longer wanted contact with those she was avoiding for whatever reason, or she was actually missing. Considering the roommate had failed to file a report, Detective Shaw guessed that this would be a quick visit with a woman who had found a new job.

He trekked down the short stretch of sidewalk, passing a tricycle missing one of its back wheels and a deflated kickball on his way to the staircase that zigzagged up the side of the building. His knees cracked as he climbed, too much time spent sitting catching up with him. Arriving at the door, he removed his sunglasses, storing them in his pocket. He swiped at the sweat on his face with a soggy paper towel, returned it to his pants pocket, and then knocked on the door.

A gush of icy air assaulted him as the door opened. He stood, staring. It took him a minute to place the face on the other side of the door frame.

"Detective Shaw! To what do I owe the pleasure?"

He cleared his throat, finding his voice. "Pam. This is . . . unexpected. I, uh, am actually here to speak with Ms. Mays."

"Oh. Well, I'm sorry, but she's not here."

"May I ask when you're expecting her back?"

"I'm not sure that she is. Coming back, I mean."

They exchanged stares. He studied her expression, large brown eyes opened wide, pudgy cheeks flush. Her hands wrestled with each other as she stood before him in the doorway.

"Why don't you come inside," she finally asked. Pam stepped back, allowing him entry. Accepting her invitation, Shaw crossed the threshold into the small apartment. The interior was old, but clean. The living room was dark, with the shades drawn and only a single lamp and the TV for illumination. He took a seat on the tan corduroy couch and was immediately accosted by a fluffy thing with long white hair. He suspected there was a cat somewhere inside the fur ball on his lap.

"Prissy, get down."

"It's ok," he lied.

Pam took a seat across from him on a well-worn recliner with a faded floral pattern that seemed to double as the cat's scratching post.

"So, how long have you lived here?"

"About three months. Betsy was nice enough to take me in when I got to town. I went to school with a cousin of hers back home."

"When did she leave?"

"About a week ago. Maybe a little more."

"And that didn't strike you as odd?"

"She said it was a long time coming. Said if she didn't follow her dreams and see the world now, she'd never get her chance."

"And she just left?"

"Uhuh. Told me to keep the apartment and all the furniture and stuff in exchange for looking after the cat."

"Do you have any idea where she went?"

"Not exactly. But I think she went out west. She was always talking about having a thing for cowboys."

"Do you have any idea if this type of behavior is out of character for her?"

"Honestly, detective, I didn't really know her before I moved here, but I imagine that it is. I mean, she had roots here. A job, friends . . . I don't know what was going on in her life, she never really opened up to me, but she just seemed . . . well, bored I guess. Dissatisfied."

"Any way I could get the contact information for that cousin of hers?"

Something about the look on Pam's face as she struggled for a reply struck Detective Shaw as odd. Instinct told him something was suspicious even before she made an excuse about having misplaced the phone number.

"I'll have to look around and find that for you. It's around here somewhere, I'm just not sure where."

He didn't press the issue, didn't even ask for a name. He simply bid her a polite farewell and made his departure. He had a feeling there'd be plenty for him to discover on his own.

*****

Detective Shaw sat hunched over his computer, the sticky plastic container of his microwave dinner perched precariously on the edge of the desk. A piece of shrapnel bounced off the back of his neck. His large hand clamped over the spot. Another piece pinged off his knuckle.

"Cut it out, will you? You're making a mess," he said without turning around.

A sunflower seed skidded onto the desk beside him.

"Hey."

"Hey."

"I mean it."

"I mean it."

"Don't start."

Wings beat the air, the parrot landing on his shoulder in a fluster of feathers. He absently raised a hand and tickled the bird on the neck.

"Aye, aye, skipper. A millionaire and his wife."

Detective Shaw couldn't help but smile to himself. Gilligan, his African Grey Parrot, had been his faithful, if not somewhat annoying, companion for over twenty years. There had even been a couple of occasions when he'd had to credit the bird with cracking a case for him.

"I don't think this will be one of those times, little buddy," he said, scrolling farther down the page he was reading. So far, the only facts he had been able to gather were that Betsy had been a responsible young woman who had held the same job and lived in the same apartment for the seven years since she had graduated college. And that she was the only child of two only children, so the cousin Pam had referenced couldn't have been a literal relation. No debt, not much of a social life, and with the loss of her parents in a car crash the year before, no known family.

Pam was proving to be even more of a conundrum. After a little inappropriate delving into her human resources file, he'd collected what he thought would be enough material to help him get a better feel for her past. He'd called the small office in Tennessee where Pam had previously worked for a little more information, only to discover that they couldn't help him. She'd only worked there four months before leaving for her current position. Yet a double check of her employment application confirmed that she had put the term for her length of employment there as ten years. A couple of fibs on an employment application were no cause for alarm, but that was a doozy.

A forwarded copy of her application with them had proven no more useful. Another lie, another dead end. And now the conflicting evidence before him. A yearbook photo of the Pam Gatsby who had attended the high school she had listed in her files. A DMV photograph of the Pam Gatsby whose driver's license matched the number on her paperwork. A third picture of a Pam Gatsby who had been employed as a forensic tech at a small ME's office in Kentucky many years before. All showed the same woman. None showed the woman he knew as Pam Gatsby.

One mystery didn't necessarily have anything to do with the other, but his gut told him the two cases were indeed intertwined. A quick check of his watch confirmed that it was too late to make any more calls that night. Pushing back from the desk, he rose slowly, making sure Gilligan kept his balance.

"Well, little buddy, it looks like we have a bit of a mess on our hands."

*****

"Hey Serge?" Detective Shaw stuck his head through the door as he knocked.

Sergeant Simmons looked up from the report she was reading. A hand absently flew up to her hair, gathered in a hasty ponytail at a stoplight on the drive in. She stopped herself, feeling foolish. Instead, she used the hand to beckon Detective Shaw into the room.

He slipped through the door, shutting it behind him, and settled into a seat across from her. For a moment he just looked at her, lost in the past. He marveled at how much she still looked like the girl he went to the academy with. The woman who, two decades ago, used to dance around his studio apartment in his t-shirt, Gilligan flapping around, waddling across the floor behind her as she taught him the theme song from his namesake program. Detective Shaw shook the memories from his mind, reminding himself why he was there.

"We've got a problem."

She was looking at him expectantly, waiting for him to elaborate.

"There's something shady about the new tech at the ME's Office."

"How shady?"

"Pitch black."

"You tell the Doc yet?"

Shaw shook his head. "I wanted to bring you in on this first. I might have to step on some toes to get to the bottom of this one."

"Whatcha got so far?"

"Her roommate is MIA. Dropped off the map, entirely out of character. Report was filed by the employer. Her story reeked, so I did a little digging. Her employment application is BS. Identity appears to be stolen. I contacted the local PD from her last few stops, just to see if she ever raised any alarms."

"And?"

"She didn't. But there's at least one person in each town with whom she was associated who went missing while she was around and who's never been seen again."

"And you're thinking?"

"I'm thinking it's too many coincidences for comfort."

"I think you're right," Sergeant Simmons said. "And I think you're definitely going to step on some toes. This is delicate, Shaw. This is a possible serial killer in our own ranks. I don't need to tell you how bad this could turn out."

"That's why I came to you. I want you in on this."

"Good," she grinned. "I just bought a new pair of boots I need to break in."

*****

Detective Shaw and Sergeant Simmons stood in silence on the back bay of the Medical Examiner's Office, waiting for Dr. Hastings to come out to speak with them. A white van backed up to the Dock, the words 'Shady Groves Funeral Home' painted tastefully in small navy block letters across the back. The driver hopped out, running up the concrete steps as fast as his wiry old legs could carry him.

"Babe!"

"Henry!" Sergeant Simmons greeted him, arms wide open. She enveloped the old man in a hug, glad to feel the muscles still hard despite the withered skin and shrinking frame. The funeral home director was one of the few old friends who could get away with calling her by her first name. "You're looking great."

"I'd like to say the same about you, but I hear it's Sergeant now, so I guess I better be careful how I say it, huh?" he grinned. "Shaw," he nodded to the detective. "It's great to see you two kids. Together," he added, wiggling his eyebrows.

"Are you here alone?" Sergeant Simmons asked, ignoring the innuendo.

"Yep. Just one pick-up today. That poor girl who lost a leg and bled out in the boating accident last week. Figured since it's a light haul, I'd handle it myself. Sent the kids to the beach to enjoy the weather while summer's still here. Doc Hastings," he said, nodding as the Chief Medical Examiner joined them. "Well, I'll let you folks get to your business. But don't you be a stranger, Babe, stop by some time for a visit. It'll do this old man some good."

"Of course, Henry. I promise. It was great seeing you." She gave his arm a squeeze.

With a wink and a grin, he opened the back doors of the van, pulled out a stretcher, and wheeled it through the doors inside.

"Does he still do pick-ups by himself often?" she asked Dr. Hastings as they watched the doors swing shut behind him.

"More since Martha passed. Usually one of the kids comes with him, though."

"Who's back there now?"

"Just Pam. Comes early, stays late, she's a real harder worker, that one. Now what's this problem you were telling me we might have?"

73

Detective Shaw and Sergeant Simmons exchanged looks.

"This is going to be bad, I can tell." Doctor Hastings wrung his hands. "Maybe we should go inside and discuss this in my office." He looked from face to face. "Crap. The problem's inside. That's why you called me to meet you out here." He adjusted his wireframe glasses, ran a hand over his sparse combover. "Well, let's get on with it then, shall we? Don't keep me in suspense."

Clearing his throat, Detective Shaw said, "I was speaking with the Human Resource Director for Criminal Justice Services. I was asking about the hiring process, how candidates are vetted, the steps of the decision making process. I was asking, in particular, about Ms. Gatsby."

Doctor Hastings nodded. "Yes, I'm afraid I did step around protocol a bit in hiring Pam, but you see, we've been shorthanded for so long, and she's a dream to work with. She's a real self-starter, willing to handle so much of the process herself. Having a tech who is comfortable opening and closing for me, well, it cuts my workload considerably. I understand that she doesn't have the education we usually require for the position, but there's something to be said about on the job training, and having spent ten years at her previous position . . ."

"That's just it, Dr. Hastings," Detective Shaw interrupted. "She wasn't at her previous position for ten years. Or her position before that.

74

Or the one before that. It seems as if Ms. Gatsby has done quite a bit of relocating."

"Damn. This is my fault. I should never have side-stepped the hiring process. So, what kind of a fallout are we talking here, detective? Are all the cases she worked on compromised?"

"I'm afraid it's a little more complicated than that, Doc. It also appears as if she's left a string of missing persons in her wake. Including her current roommate."

"You're kidding."

Shaw shook his head.

Dr. Hastings wobbled over to the steps and took a seat. "This is serious. And it's my fault. This is . . . this is a career ender." He looked up at Detective Shaw and Sergeant Simmons. "Forgive me for being so callous, I realize the ramifications of this are immense. But my career . . . I mean, could I face jail time for this?"

Sergeant Simmons joined the man on the steps. His face was grey, his body trembling. "That certainly isn't our intention," she said. "Nothing has been proven yet, the investigation is just beginning. We're telling you because we wanted to extend the professional courtesy of including you in the loop. But we will need your full cooperation."

"Of course. I appreciate it, Sergeant. Detective."

The back door of the building popped open as Henry wheeled the gurney out, a black bag strapped securely in place. He struggled to get the stretcher over the doorsill. Detective Shaw rushed to his assistance.

"Thanks," Henry said, removing a handkerchief from his pocket and mopping at the sweat on his brow. "I guess maybe I'm getting a little old to be doing this on my own."

Concerned, Sergeant Simmons stood. "Why don't you come take a seat for a minute and catch your breath, Henry? Detective Shaw and I can handle loading the van."

"Maybe I will," Henry said, face crimson with exertion. "Just for a minute."

Sergeant Simmons took Henry's place at the head of the stretcher and gave it a push. Brows furrowed, she shifted her grip and lifted her end of the gurney. "Hmm. Henry? This the girl from the boating accident?"

"Yep."

"What's she scheduled for? Open casket?"

"Nope. Cremation. Why?"

She didn't answer. Exchanging a look with Detective Shaw, she took the bag's zipper in hand and pulled. "Dr. Hastings, I'm afraid we're going to need your assistance."

*****

Sergeant Simmons and Detective Shaw wheeled the gurney back into the building, down the hall, and into the autopsy suite. Dr. Hastings took his time as he followed, his slow steps betraying his reluctance. Henry brought up the rear, hoping he'd be included in on the action.

Pam stared at the group wide eyed as they returned with the stretcher. She distanced herself until her back was against the wall. There was no chance of escape. She watched with growing dread as they suited up, donning booties and gloves and the aprons that Dr. Hastings handed out. Detective Shaw crossed the room, approaching the puffy cheeked woman.

"Ms. Gatsby," he said, drawing her attention away from the black bag strapped to the stretcher. "You're under arrest for suspicion of murder."

He read her Miranda rights as Dr. Hastings locked the gurney in place, undid the fetters and unzipped the full length of the bag. He stumbled back a step, and then turned to look at Pam, giving her a long, hard stare before returning to the victim before him.

"Dr. Hastings," Sergeant Simmons said, her voice filling the room. "Was the leg that was lost in the boating accident ever recovered?"

"No."

"Then whose leg is it that has been sewed onto the deceased?"

"I have no idea."

Henry leaned in for a better view. The leg that had been crudely sewed onto the dead girl was a little longer and larger, with a slight variation in color, but would not have raised an alarm had he seen it while handling the corpse at the crematorium. He would have assumed that the difference in the limb had been caused by the injury, submersion, and decomposition process. He said so aloud.

"I believe we'll be able to match the extra leg with a certain missing roommate. What do you think Ms. Gatsby?" Detective Shaw asked.

If Pam heard his words, it didn't register in her vacant stare.

"Dr. Hastings, would you be so kind as to open her up?"

"Excuse me?"

"I have reason to believe that there may be additional contents in the deceased's organ bag," Detective Shaw explained.

Dr. Hastings gave a low moan, a sound heavy with the remorse that he had let such atrocities happen under his care. Within moments he had cut through the seam and reopened the body cavity. Removing the bag from within, he set it carefully in a pan on the counter. By the weight of the sack, he knew the detective was right, yet as he cut it open, he wasn't prepared for the gruesome sight that was revealed.

"Well, we have dentals."

*****

Sergeant Simmons sat on the white porch steps. A chill breeze crisped the air, heralding the impending fall of summer. Taking a sip of lemonade, she looked up at her companions and smiled.

Detective Shaw leaned against the porch railing, face to the sun. Henry rocked lazily in an old oak rocking chair, an equally old hound dog lying at his feet.

"So, this is it," Henry said. The dog lifted his head and cocked an ear at his master's voice. "Retirement."

As if understanding the word, the dog settled his chin back on his paws and closed his eyes.

"Never thought I'd see the day," Detective Shaw said.

"Well, I'm an old man, and it's a strange world. Getting stranger by the day. Figured I might as well quit while I'm ahead. You'd a told me five years ago that the chaos would hit so close to home, I would have gone and retired then." He shook his head, clucking in disapproval. "That Pam, she seemed like a nice enough lady. Never would have guessed her for a killer. That's bad enough. But to get rid of her victims by putting parts of them inside other people? Working at the ME's Office so she could sew up the evidence inside of unsuspecting dead folk? That's madness, and I'm just too old for it. This world's taken a nasty turn. You two have your work cut out for you."

Detective Shaw and Sergeant Simmons looked at each other and smiled.

It's In The Bag first appeared in *The Dark Lane Anthology*, volume 5

Searching for Sunshine

Michelle had been numb since she received the phone call three days ago. She'd made the four-hour drive home without shedding a tear, for surely she had been told wrong. She had misunderstood, it was as simple as that, and there was no need to get upset over a silly mistake. They'd all have a laugh when she got home and told everyone what she thought she had heard.

When she was forced to park along the road because the drive was packed with cars, Michelle wasn't scared. She had smiled and thought what a great deal of fuss they had gone to in order to get her home for a party. After entering the house and pressing her way through the throng of black clad mourners in search of her mother, only to find her curled in a corner on the floor of her parent's bedroom, drenched in her own tears, Michelle still wasn't worried. Her mother should have gone to

Hollywood, she should have been an actress and won an Oscar for her betrayal of a grief-stricken mother.

That they'd managed to keep the act up for three days was of no concern. She came from a long line of stubborn people. Mule was in her blood. The cemetery had been a bit much, though. The way her father's knees had buckled as they lowered the tiny coffin into the ground, her mom, who had been leaning on him for support, collapsing to the earth, gathering handfuls of dirt and grass in her hands as she wailed a sound of pure torment, well, that had been overdoing it.

That was when Michelle decided she'd had enough. Walking the three miles from the graveyard to the house along streets lined with trees in full late spring bloom, she breathed in the fragrance of lilac, listened to the hum of happy bees. The house was empty when she got there.

Climbing the stairs, she let herself into her sister's room and sat on the end of the bed. It was too quiet. The air was too still, as if time had frozen and the molecules in the room were motionless instead of colliding off each other in constant action.

Smiling, Michelle leaned over and grabbed the limp stuffed bunny with floppy ears from the head of the bed. "Amelia, I'm in your ro-om," she said in a singsong voice. "I've got Mr. Flopsie. I'm going to do bad things to him."

Like a twig snapping underfoot her grief broke at that moment, all the unfelt feelings from the last few days bombarding her at once. Her body shook violently under the waves of sorrow, tsunamis of tears bursting relentlessly from eyes that quickly swelled from the violence of her crying. Michelle wept until she was empty. Then she curled up on her sister's bed, Mr. Flopsie clutched to her chest by both arms, and she slept.

*****

When she woke, Michelle knew that other people were in the house. Creeping to the door, she locked it. Leaning her back against the barricade, she slid down to the floor, Mr. Flopsie still clenched in her fist.

She hadn't had time for it. Her sister's last call. The phone had rung, she had answered it, and upon discovering that it was her little sister she had rushed her off the phone and ended the call. Rudely. Carelessly. And now she was going to have to live with it. Not knowing what it was her sister had wanted to say. Never having the chance to hear the voice that flowed like warm honey in the sun again.

It hadn't always been easy, having a sister that was eight years younger. She'd asked her parents for a sibling when she was four; had gotten one when she was eight. At nineteen, as a freshman in college, Michelle was understandably busy.

Only, the lack of time was a mess of her own making, not from the demands of her course load. Or what would have been the demands of her course load, had she not spent too much time partying and chasing boys and sleeping late instead of going to class. Now the semester was coming to an end and her grades were not what they should be.

Not that her parents would notice now, with Amelia gone. They wouldn't have been mad, anyway, they would have been sympathetic, feeling bad that Michelle was having difficulties achieving the same grades she was used to earning, wondering if her pride was hurt by this academic slight, if her ego was bruised. And for this – this silly, trivial thing, this ridiculous excuse for a piss poor reason, Michelle would never know what it was that Amelia had wanted so badly to tell her.

Michelle looked down at the bunny in her hand. She sat Mr. Flopsie on her knees, ran her fingertips over his worn velvet ears, straightened his frayed navy coat, tugged at a frazzled string that poked out from where one of the buttons was missing. Even just last year, Amelia wouldn't have been caught without Mr. Flopsie by her side. He was her faithful companion, the best friend of a little girl who was too painfully shy to make many real friends. It still seemed so unreal, so impossible.

Hot tears seared through the eyelids she had squeezed shut against them. Amelia knew better, dammit! She was an excellent swimmer. Michelle had taught her herself. It was their thing. Had been, she reminded herself. Was.

Amelia swam like a dolphin, she was born for the water, but she never would have tried swimming in the retention pond out back, Michelle was sure of it. Years ago, she had told Amelia that was where all the toilets in the neighborhood drained to. Michelle had told her it was a pond of poo, and Amelia had believed her.

Michelle knew with every cell of her body that Amelia had not willingly entered the murky ditch water of that deep, manmade hole. She also knew what the alternative meant. But who would listen to her? It didn't matter, she decided. She had to try. Someone had murdered her little sister and they were damn sure going to pay for it.

Sharp pain lanced through her stomach with the heat of fiery red pokers. Grimacing, she focused on the sensation, feeling every ounce of the hurt tenfold. She deserved it.

The door vibrated against her back as someone tapped against the other side. Michelle scooted away on her knees, turned to stare at this sign of life, briefly seeing an image of the grim reaper come to drag her off to the depths of hell. Maybe she deserved that, too.

"Michelle?"

Her mother's voice carried through the door, the mere sound conjuring love and warmth. Though she knew she should deny herself the comfort, Michelle scrambled on her knees to the door and opened it.

"Mommy."

If her mother heard the word, she did not acknowledge it. Elizabeth Farley slipped through the threshold as if chased by her own demons. She rested her back against the door a moment, eyes closed, lips moving silently; whether prayer or plea, Michelle did not know.

Opening her eyes, she smiled down at Michelle, ran a soft palm over her damp cheek. Then the spell was broken. She removed Mr. Flopsie from Michelle's hand, the hand that clutched at her hips like a small child begging to be picked up, and carried the toy back to the bed, placing him reverently back onto the pillow.

Michelle watched as her mother crossed the room to the window. Watched as Elizabeth Farley stared vacantly through the glass panes for several moments before yanking the curtains closed. Watched as her eyes fell to the desk centered below the window. She straightened several objects on the desktop, a small smile forming on her lips.

"She was going through a Harriet the Spy stage, just like you did." Elizabeth spun to look at Michelle abruptly, like she could no longer face the memories behind her. "You should come downstairs, honey. Your father needs you. We all do."

A clipped sound of grief strangled inside her throat and she hurried out of the room. Michelle stared after her for a moment, then felt her eyes drawn to the curtained window like they'd been snared by a fishhook. A sliver of light winked from between the curtain panels.

Michelle didn't need to look out the window to see the view. She knew her sister's room overlooked the retention pond around which the houses in the neighborhood were built, like a rotten core, the dark, filthy waters that had snatched Amelia's life in the center.

Sighing deeply, Michelle forced herself to leave the room, each step down the stairs a battle against herself. She slipped into the realm of the mourning unnoticed, weaving in and out of the groups, lingering at the edges of each cluster only long enough to know that she didn't belong.

Finding her dad in the kitchen, she pressed herself into a corner, trying to provide support, but after only ten minutes she couldn't handle the pain reflecting in his watery, tear filled eyes. Seeking escape, Michelle tiptoed through the house until she reached the front door. She spilled herself into the fresh air, relief filling her lungs with each breath.

Settling onto the steps, she rested her head against the porch railing and stared down the street. They lived on a relatively quiet stretch. Most of the families with young children lived on the far side of the retention pond, on the opposite side of the street. The Farley's neighbors were of a quiet type, retirees, childless professional couples, a lone bachelor or two. Michelle's eyes roved over each house, searching for a sign, a secret, anything that would help make Amelia's death make sense.

Her mother had said Amelia had been going through a spy phase. Had Amelia snooped on the wrong person? Had she discovered something about one of these people that had resulted in the tragedy that now clung to Michelle, new pains snaring her with every thought like the sticky filaments of a spider's web?

Michelle didn't notice the stranger's approach until his shoe scuffed against the concrete walk only feet from where she sat. Jumping, her heart pulsed violently against the base of her throat. She stared at the man, wide eyes shrinking to slits as an unaccountable anger grew within her at his intrusion.

"I'm sorry, I didn't mean to disturb you." The man smiled down at her, his face kind, his eyes sympathetic without being condescending. That his very manner made the pain within her want to quell a bit when she did not deserve a reprieve made Michelle even angrier. She watched warily as he sat on the far side of the stoop. "Doesn't seem right, that the day should be so nice at a time like this."

Michelle bit her lower lip to keep it from trembling, digging her fingernails deep into the flesh of her palms to keep from crying, because he was right. It wasn't fair. The sun shouldn't be shining; the sky shouldn't be blue. The day should be dark and gray and stormy, like her heart.

"I'm Detective Shaw."

Michelle's face jerked to face him with a start. He remained facing forward, glancing at her sideways.

"You're Michelle Farley, right? Amelia's sister."

Michelle answered by crossing her arms over her chest, sharpening her eyes at him.

"I'm the detective in charge of investigating what happened to your sister."

Michelle felt her body puff up, filled with a breath she couldn't release. She hadn't known that Amelia's death was being investigated. No one had told her.

"Listen, I know that right now isn't the time for me to be bothering you. I just stopped by today to pay my respects. But if it's possible, when you're ready, I'd like to talk to you."

He withdrew a card from his inside jacket pocket and handed it to her. Michelle stared at it for a moment before her hand mechanically reached out and took it, crushing it inside her clenched fist.

"I'm having a hard time understanding why Amelia would have gone into the retention pond. And I've been told that she was a strong swimmer, that you taught her yourself. Like I said, when you're ready, I'd like to talk to you. There's a lot that doesn't make sense that I could use your help with."

Michelle rose to her feet as if pulled by invisible wires. She nodded at the detective, not trusting her voice to speak. Her mind was a jumble of conflicting thoughts, elation that maybe she was right, that Amelia's death was not an accident, yet horrified by what that meant. She walked woodenly into the house, up the stairs and into Amelia's room. She could feel the detective's eyes on her back long after she had locked the door behind her.

*****

The light was weird, fuzzy and filtered, weak, wavering. She was under water. Michelle opened her mouth to scream but found that she was breathing just fine. The water held her in a comforting embrace. This was where she belonged.

Amelia's face floated above her, eyes closed in the peace of sleep. Her golden hair drifted outward like rays of the sun, a celestial corona, a crown of sunshine, a circle of light emanating from her peaceful expression. Amelia's eyes opened. They found Michelle's through the hazy depths. They were so full of love, so tender. Michelle reached her hand towards her sister, wanting to pull her into her arms.

Amelia's eyes flashed. Panic stretched her features tight. Her arms flailed, hands finding her throat as she struggled to breathe. Bubbles of air clouded the water between them. Michelle fought to move forward, to find her sister through the frothy maelstrom.

Then the water was once again crystal clear. Amelia's eyes were still on hers, only now they were red, full of sadness and sorrow. Her lips pulsed like a fish gasping for air. She spasmed in violent jerks. Michelle cried, her heart breaking as she wrestled against the water, trying to reach her sister. Amelia's eyes closed in a series of heavy-lidded blinks, like she was falling asleep.

Michelle released a silent scream as her sister hovered above her, dead. Suddenly, Amelia's eyes flew open. She pushed her arm towards Michelle, pointing a finger at her, and opened her mouth, screaming. The sound shattered the water. It fell away in torrential gushes.

Michelle struggled to remain upright, searching for Amelia, needing her sister, but she was nowhere to be found. When Michelle woke, she discovered that the dampness she felt was from the tear drenched pillow.

*****

The aftereffects of the dream were far worse than any hangover Michelle had ever had. As soon as the sun lightened the sky she struggled out of bed. Amelia's bed. She put Mr. Flopsie back on the pillow and smoothed the sheets before slipping down the hall to her own room.

She skipped a shower, instead favoring a departure made before her parents woke. Changing her clothes, she shoved her wallet into the back pocket of her jeans, her cellphone into the other, grabbed a hoodie and headed for the stairs. She paused outside of Amelia's room.

Pushing the door open, it was there, wadded on the floor, like it was waiting for her. Michelle snatched the detective's card up and shoved it into her front pocket. Creeping down the stairs and out the front door, Michelle shivered and pulled on the sweatshirt. Today wasn't going to be as nice as yesterday. Today was going to match her mood.

She debated taking her car, but instead chose a long walk to help clear her head. A part of her relished the idea of the punishment of being caught in bad weather. The other part simply didn't care.

By the time she'd walked the five miles to the Waverly Police Department headquarters, what little light the sky had held had leaked away. The wind lashed at the world in a fury, ripping leaves off trees and hurling them into the gray void of the sky. Michelle hesitated on the steps of the station, then was driven inside by the force of a frigid gust against her back.

She blinked against the sudden brightness of the florescent lights. Despite the early hour, there was a flourish of activity already underway behind the Plexiglas partition that separated the lounge from the squad room. A receptionist, or maybe it was an officer, looked up from a desk behind the divider. She smiled at Michelle from behind the thick glass and shifted closer to the grate as she said, "May I help you?"

Michelle's voice wavered as she spoke. "I'm here to speak with Detective Shaw."

"Is he expecting you?"

"I'm not sure. Maybe."

"Let me try his line and we'll see if he's in."

The lady spun her chair towards a complicated looking phone base and picked up the receiver. Though Michelle strained to hear what was being said, she could not catch a word. After what seemed like an absurdly long time, the woman set the phone down and turned towards Michelle, again with the smile.

"He'll be right out."

Michelle tried to force a smile back towards the lady, but it felt wrong, too big for her face. She nodded and pretended to read a poster on the wall about drug use statistics. All too soon the door opened, and she found herself standing in Detective Shaw's shadow.

"Michelle, I'm glad you came." His tone was sincere, and she felt her skin warming under the glow of his steady blue eyes. "Why don't you come in and sit so we can talk."

Michelle nodded and followed him through the door to the other side. She couldn't help but to stare curiously at the people working behind the desks that they passed. People trying to do things that were good. Like finding the monsters that murder little girls.

"Can I get you something to drink? Coffee? Water?"

Michelle shook her head, then followed him through another door. He closed it behind her. She had expected a stark room, cold, plain, with a metal table and chairs like on TV. What she found instead was a small room cluttered with papers, dark wood bookcases and desk, and cushy leather chairs.

Detective Shaw gestured for her to take a seat. She sank deep into the folds of the cushions. Instead of rounding the desk to sit behind it, he took the chair beside hers.

Michelle stared at her hands, not knowing where to begin. Suddenly, the words she didn't know had been waiting spewed forward, filling the space between them. "Who do you think killed my sister?"

Detective Shaw sat straighter in the chair. "You don't mince words, do you?"

She tried focusing on him through tears that clouded her eyes.

"Listen, Michelle, I know how this is. And I know that sometimes it makes things like this easier if there's someone to blame. But that's not always the case."

His words struck Michelle like a slap. Shaking her head, she said, "What do you mean? I thought you were investigating her murder?"

Detective Shaw slipped his hand over Michele's, where it gripped the arm of the chair. His touch was light and warm, his skin rough. "I'm investigating Amelia's death. I never said murder."

She looked down at his hand, covering her own. He gave it a small squeeze and withdrew back to his own space. She looked up slowly, purposefully, locking his gaze under her own. "Then what do you think happened?"

Detective Shaw pursed his lips, staring hard at Michelle, trying to decide what to tell her. He settled on the truth. "I think that sometimes situations get out of hand and bad things happen. I think that your sister was playing with some other kids, maybe being bullied by them, and things went too far."

"Amelia didn't really have many friends."

"Do you know if she was being bullied by anyone?"

"No."

"Would she have told you if she was?"

Michelle thought about her sister's phone call, the subject forever to remain unknown, and whispered, "I don't know."

"Do you think it's a possible scenario?"

"Maybe. But even if it's not, you have questions. You don't believe that it was just an accident." Her words were a statement, not a question. "And you're right. Someone killed my sister, Detective. Don't ask me how I know. There are a million reasons that would make me think this wasn't an accident, but that's not it. I don't think. I know. Every cell in my body knows. And I want whoever did this to be found and pay for what they've done."

Detective Shaw studied her for a moment. He nodded. "Fair enough. If you believe it that strongly, that's good enough for me. Is there anyone you suspect?"

"No. But I think that it may have been one of our neighbors. My mom said that Amelia was going through a Harriet the Spy stage. I did the same thing when I was around her age, and at that age the only people you get to snoop on are the neighbors."

"But you don't suspect anyone in particular?"

"No. I've been gone for most of the last year, at college. But two people moved in during the summer. Everyone else has been in the neighborhood for years."

Detective Shaw stood and grabbed a pen and a pad of paper off his desk. Settling back into his chair, he gestured for Michelle to continue.

"A man moved next door, our neighbor to the right when you're facing the house. Gary. But I'm not sure if that's a first or a last name."

The detective nodded as he scribbled on the paper.

"And a lady moved in two houses further down from him. I'm not sure what her name is, but it's Mrs. Burke's old house."

"I'll start with them," he said, looking up and focusing his surreally blue eyes back on her. "But there's a few questions I'd like to ask you, first."

"Shoot."

"Your parents said that you taught Amelia to swim. When was that?"

"I was in junior high. Seventh grade, thirteen, so Amelia would have been five."

"Did you take her swimming a lot?"

"Oh, yeah." Michelle nodded. "I wanted to make it onto the swim team when I got to high school, so I practiced, like, every day. That was the year my mom went back to work. I had to watch Amelia. Her preschool was between my school and the Y, where I practiced, so I'd pick her up every day on my way."

"What kind of swimmer was she?"

"A natural. Much better than I was at her age. Better than I am now, except that she lacks focus and a competitive nature. Lacked." Michelle's voice trailed away.

Detective Shaw gave her a moment alone with her thoughts before asking, "What about the retention pond?"

"What about it?"

"You two ever talk about it?"

"What do you mean?"

"I grew up in a house that bordered a drainage pond, just like yours. My older brother used to tell me there was pirate treasure at the bottom to trick me into it. I used to tell my little sister that an alligator lived in it to keep her away from it. You two have anything like that?"

"Yeah." A smile broke Michelle's face, the first in days. Strangely, it didn't feel wrong. "We did. I told her that the pond was where all the sewage from the neighborhood went. We called it Poo Pond."

"Nice one."

Michelle nodded, holding onto to the smile a second longer before she let it join the memories she was storing away.

"So, there was little chance Amelia would willingly decide to swim in there." He wrote on his notepad, the pen making a long series of whispered scratches across the paper.

"Now you have to answer some of my questions."

Detective Shaw looked up, surprised. "Okay," he said, his tone wary.

"You ever handled a murder investigation before?"

Waverly was an upper middle-class town known for its relative lack of crime, but it brushed against Boston on its far end, and several less fortunate towns nestled in its shadow. Detective Shaw thought it was a fair question.

"More than I'd like to admit. Waverly picks up all the major crimes cases for Lexingham and Starborough, and I work with the Boston PD on occasion. Homicide investigations comprise about 90% of my case load."

Michelle nodded her approval. "You any good?"

Detective Shaw wanted to respond with a snappy comeback, a funny retort like his clients have never complained, but he bit his tongue. Instead, he gave Michelle his most serious expression and said, "Yes. Yes, I am."

"Good."

"Anything else?"

"Yeah. What is it that you know about this that I don't?"

"What makes you think I know something you don't?"

"This was too easy. I came in here and told you that my dead sister was murdered and instead of trying to convince me of all the reasons why you think that's not true, you listened to me and agreed to investigate it. You wouldn't have jumped on board so easily unless there was something that made you agree with me."

Memories of the autopsy flashed through Detective Shaw's mind. The thin, too pale body of a dead child. Bruises that couldn't be explained. A spiral fracture to the right radius. He swallowed the memory deep into the dark pit where he kept such things.

"You knew your sister better than anyone else. The way you came in here, the confidence you had, the complete lack of doubt . . . it's common for loved ones to want a reason for their loss. But in that grappling for a cause, there's also a lot of straw grabbing, backpedaling, a lot of questions. You don't have that. You're completely sure, almost like you may have seen something."

"I had a dream," Michelle admitted. "About the pond. I had already suspected that she'd been murdered. Amelia was an excellent swimmer and she never would have gone into that pond willingly. In the dream, I was at the bottom. I watched Amelia drown, but she was pointing and screaming. There was something that was terrifying her. Amelia wasn't like that. For a little kid, there wasn't much she was scared of. I had never seen her react like that to something, not while she was alive. That just cemented it for me. I knew that something bad happened to my sister."

Michelle wiped at the tickle on her cheek with the back of her hand, smearing the tears she hadn't realized were there.

"Michelle, I'm sorry."

"Yeah, well, prove it. Find out who killed my sister."

*****

Michelle stood in Amelia's room, staring out of the window, her hand absentmindedly playing with the spyglass sitting on the corner of Amelia's desk. The water of the retention pond was black and foreboding under the cloudy sky, the wind raising tiny ripples across its surface. Her eyes seared into her neighbor's houses, trying to burn through to the secrets held within.

Despite the bad weather, several neighbors were out in their yards. The new guy, Gary something from next-door, was chopping at a patch of earth in the back corner with a garden hoe. Michelle looked down at her hand as if realizing for the first time what it held. Lifting the spyglass to her eye, she adjusted the focus with her other hand until the neighbor came into clear view.

An empty bag of topsoil lay limp at his feet as he worked the rich dirt into the native soil with the garden hoe. Maybe he was going to plant a garden. Or maybe he was up to something more suspicious. She made a note to take a walk around the pond later to get a closer look at what he was doing, then she moved on.

Mr. Charles was sitting in a chair on his back patio, staring at an empty doghouse before him. His brittle figure slumped in the chair like a defeated scarecrow. Michelle could remember back when his wife was still alive, when their children would bring the grandkids over to play.

One of them had been her age, a girl named Sarah. They used to walk Mr. Charles's dog around the neighborhood together. Then his wife had died, the kids had stopped coming over, and all Mr. Charles had left was the dog.

Now, apparently, the dog had abandoned him, too. Michelle vaguely remembered passing signs posted to trees offering a reward for the missing dog on her walks. Poor Mr. Charles. Michelle adverted her eyes to the next house.

She hadn't a clue about the lady who had moved in next to Mr. Charles, except that Mrs. Burke used to live there. Michelle had taken piano lessons from Mrs. Burke in the second grade. She spent a year of Tuesdays perched on a corner of the crowded piano bench, her fingers pressing keys under the watchful presence of Mr. Burke, whose remains sat in an urn on top of the upright.

Anytime she smelled dry cat food it reminded her of Mrs. Burke's breath and the cluttered house with the weathered piano and its spectral companion. The lessons had stopped after her parents had been invited in to hear her play. The reason why had never been discussed.

Mrs. Burke had been a weird one, sweet and generally harmless, but weird nonetheless. After living in her house over twenty years, she left without a word to any of her neighbors. Personally, Michelle didn't blame her for leaving in secret and avoiding all the fuss. But if she had known how the new owner was going to neglect her prized flower beds, the once colorful perennial gardens now choked with weeds, only an anemic flash of color straggling here and there among the dead brambles, well, Mrs. Burke might not have sold at all.

The new owner also seemed to never work. Every time Michelle caught a glimpse of her, she was lounging around with a drink in her hand. Even today, when the odds of a stray ray of sun fighting its way through the thick jumble of angry clouds overhead were slim, she lay draped over a lounge chair, sunglasses on and cocktail in hand like she was on a beach in Tahiti.

Michelle turned from the window and set the spyglass down. Peeping at the neighbors wasn't going to help her find her sister's killer. She cracked the door to Amelia's room and stuck her head out into the hall, listening to the sounds of the house. Silence bombarded her like a swarm of angry bees.

Satisfied that she was alone, she went downstairs to the kitchen. The last thing she felt like doing was eating, but it was the only way to quell the acidic burning that had rooted deep inside her chest. She tucked a knee under her as she sat at the kitchen table. Grabbing a banana from the bowl, she peeled the skin back and took a bite, rolling the mush around her mouth methodically before swallowing.

Michelle pulled the stack of mail that sat on the table closer and leafed through the envelopes, feeling a rush of anger at the bills she saw. It wasn't fair that her parents were forced to go on doing everyday mundane things like paying bills. If felt like time should stop, if only for a while. They should be allowed to take a time out, to catch their breath after the loss of their daughter.

The last letter in the pile didn't look like a bill, though. It looked like a check. Unfortunately, it wasn't addressed to either of her parents.

Michelle turned the envelope in her hands. It was addressed to Mrs. Burke, ironic since she'd just been thinking about her. The return address was the Social Security Administration. Suspecting the letter might be important, Michelle wondered if the new owner of Mrs. Burke's house would have a forwarding address for her. Even if she didn't, asking would provide Michelle with the perfect excuse to introduce herself to the stranger who was always home. Maybe the lady had seen or heard something that could help Michelle discover what had happened to her sister.

Rising from the table, Michelle tossed her banana peel in the trash and went out the back door, letter in hand. She walked across the yard, past the cedar planked privacy fence that ran between each neighbor's yard, and into the thicker grass that grew around the bank of the retention pond. Her feet sunk deep into the waterlogged soil, the mud sucking at her shoes with each step. Even though the grass had been tamped down by a dozen feet, the cops and paramedics and investigators who had fished her sister's body out of the dark green waters of the pond, Michelle imagined that she could see the smaller prints of her sister's shoes leading her forward.

Michelle's skin tingled as she walked past the yard next door. The Gary guy had gone inside, but the area where he'd been working was marked by a patch of dark, grassless earth torn open like a gaping wound. Her nose twitched, wrinkling against the awful stench that hung heavy in the air. It smelled like something had died here. Like the garden was a disguise for a grave. The hair on the back of her neck raised. Michelle suddenly felt exposed and vulnerable. Glancing towards the house, she thought she saw a shadow behind the window, watching her.

Quickening her steps, she hurried until she passed the barrier and walked along the rim of the pond bordering Mr. Charles's yard, promising herself she'd call Detective Shaw as soon as she got back to let him know about the neighbor's suspicious gardening activities.

Mr. Charles still sat where she had seen him, staring at the doghouse. He looked up at her, raised a hand in the air to wave. A leash was clutched in his fingers. Michelle paused.

She could feel the pain of the old man's loss palpitating through the air, an echo of her own hurt. She walked up the slight incline of the yard until she was standing next to the doghouse. Resting a hand lightly upon the pitched roof, Michelle said, "She was a good dog."

The old man grimaced in what may have supposed to have been a smile. "She was. Until she decided to run off."

Michelle pictured the Golden Retriever in her mind, the sun sparking off her honeyed fur as the dog ran on a random summer day, and smiled.

"Sorry about your sister. She was a good kid."

The smile slipped from Michelle's face as she nodded.

"She'd been a big help to me of late. Helped exercise the dog for me, played with her and took her for walks. Did us both a lot of good." His voice broke as a sob bubbled up in his throat. "Don't know what kind of world it is, little girls dying and old dogs running off. Not sure it's a place I want to be anymore."

"Do you have any idea what happened? With the dog, I mean."

He squinted at her with rheumy, red-ringed eyes and said, "It's the darndest thing. She never left the yard, not unless she was on a leash. There were some paw prints down by the pond. Don't know what possessed her to take off. Your sister was just as heartbroken as I was. She's the one who put the signs up for me. She spent hours down there looking at the prints, trying to track where the dog went, but I guess she never did find out."

Something twitched just beneath the surface of Michelle's skin, a physical manifestation of a thought. "Which way did the prints lead?" she asked.

"That way." He raised a skeletal arm that hung like a leafless twig as it quivered in the air. "The way you were heading. But like I said, there mustn't have been much of a trail to follow."

Michelle nodded and forced a swallow past what felt like a stone lodged in her throat. "Well, I'll keep an eye out for her."

Mr. Charles nodded, his arm dropping. His eyes returned to the doghouse, as if staring into its depth would reveal what had happened to his dog.

Michelle turned and retreated to the shore of the pond. She wasn't sure if the tumult in her stomach was good or bad. She had a feeling that Amelia's death was somehow related to the dog, that if she could solve the mystery surrounding the dog's disappearance, it would lead her to her sister's killer.

A shrill scream carried over the pond through the settling dusk, startling Michelle.

Another shriek sounded, followed by the sound of children's laughter. Thinking about Detective Shaw's theory, she shivered.

The faint odor of decay carried over from the neighbor's new garden. The smell of death and a missing dog. A child's death would be harder to conceal, unless, of course, you made it look like an accident and didn't try. The nerves in her arms tingled so bad that they itched. Staring down at the letter clutched in her hand, she decided to finish what she had set out to do before calling Detective Shaw.

She slogged through the muck until she reached the next yard. She watched the motionless woman on the lawn chair for a minute, waiting for the woman to notice her, but with the dark sunglasses on, Michelle couldn't even tell if she was awake. She crept forward a few feet, sliding her feet noisily across the grass. Still nothing. Clearing her throat, Michelle said, "Excuse me? Ma'am?"

A forearm moved languidly to the woman's brow, as if she were shielding her eyes from the absent sun in order to see Michelle. Shifting her weight, the woman struggled to sit up in the chair.

"Yeah?"

"My name is Michelle Farley. I live a few houses down."

The woman tipped her sunglasses down her nose with one finger and starred over the frames at Michelle.

"I, um, a piece of mail for Mrs. Burke was delivered to my house by mistake. She was, uh, the woman who used to live here. I was just wondering if you had a forwarding address for her."

The woman's face relaxed into a welcoming smile. Swinging her legs to the side, she rose from the chair, gesturing for Michelle to come closer. "Well, aren't you sweet. Sure, honey, I have her new address inside. Might take me a moment to find it, though, so why don't you come inside and let me pour you a glass of tea while you wait?"

She didn't wait for Michelle to reply, instead walking into the house and leaving the sliding door to the patio open behind her. Michelle hurried to catch up, entering the darkened house. She was immediately struck with a chill, the hair on her arms standing on end. The woman stood next to a table just inside the door.

"I'm Carly, by the way. What did you say your name was?"

"Michelle."

"Mind if I smoke, Michelle?"

The cigarette was lit before Michelle had a chance to answer.

"Sit for a minute."

Michelle pulled a chair back from the table and sat, careful not to touch the thick dust that coated the table. Time seemed to lag, actions caught in slow motion as she watched Carly ash her cigarette in an urn on the far side of the table. The vessel looked strangely familiar.

"What can I get you to drink?"

"Oh, nothing, thank you. Just Mrs. Burke's new address. I really ought to be getting home soon."

"That the letter, there?" Carly tipped her cigarette towards the envelope in Michelle's hand.

"Yes."

"I'm not quite sure where I put that address. Why don't you leave it here with me and I'll forward it to Mrs. Burke for you?"

"No, that's okay." Michelle tried not to look around the house. She kept her eyes on Carly's, a blank expression on her face. "I don't mind waiting."

Michelle realized why the urn looked familiar, why, in fact, she recognized everything in the house. Her foot pumped nervously under the table, adrenaline surging through limbs that planned to run as soon as Carly left the room.

"I thought you had to get home."

Michelle jumped to her feet, unable to sit still any longer.

"You're right, I do. I'll tell you what, I'll come back for the address later."

Carly lurched in front of the door, blocking Michelle's exit. She slid the lock. When she looked up at Michelle, her eyes appeared black. "I'm afraid that's not going to work for me."

*****

Clouds tumbled against each other overhead like a pack of fighting dogs. Detective Shaw squinted up at a sky smeared with the colors of a bruise, then, shaking his head, pulled the scuba tank out of the back of his Jeep and shut the hatch. He was officially on unofficial business, which meant that his time to attend to the task at hand was limited. Night, with its intent to shroud the world, was coming fast.

Since the Medical Examiner, a retiring pathologist who hadn't wanted to end his career with an unclosed case, had decided to put accidental drowning on Amelia's death certificate instead of undetermined drowning, despite there being questions surrounding the manner of her death, the Waverly Police Department would not pay for an underwater forensic team to dive the scene. Detective Shaw had requested the underwater search after the autopsy had revealed unexplained bruising and the broken arm. Spiral fractures don't happen from flailing against something in a struggle to stay afloat; they happen when someone grabs a child's arm too roughly and pulls.

After hearing Michelle describe her dream about her sister in the pond, it was something that he knew had to be done. Even if it meant him renting dive gear and trying to poorly reenact what he learned on a trip to the Florida Keys over fifteen years ago.

Strapping the tank on his back, he duck-walked over the sidewalk and across a random yard to the retention pond. The water, usually dark, appeared pitch black under the stormy sky. Detective Shaw tested the regulator and waded into the algae laden liquid before he could change his mind.

Something about this case had gotten under his skin and eaten away at the carefully constructed layer of detachment he had worked so hard to form. Turning on his dive light, Detective Shaw kicked off the sludgy bottom, his feet leaving the safety on the earth as he propelled himself deep into the inky depths of the pond.

If this dive didn't produce results, and he doubted it would, well, he wasn't quite sure what his next move would be. There were no leads to go on. There wasn't even a consensus on the suspicion surrounding the case, just a feeling deep in the pit of his gut that soured everything he forced himself to eat. His gut was never wrong.

But he had no suspects, had been unable to determine anyone who would have wanted to hurt the girl, and if he didn't get lucky, and soon, her killer would get away with the crime. Detective Shaw kicked harder, his momentum fueled by anger. The meager beam of his dive light barely cut through the murky water. He couldn't see anything, couldn't even tell if he was swimming in the right direction.

The icy fingers of panic tickled his spine. He had known this dive was a bad idea, his gut had told him this as well, but he had chosen to ignore it. Desperation, anger, hubris, they'd all fade into oblivion with him if he didn't keep his cool and resurface from the dive.

He treads water, waving the light around, searching for an answer in the dark. The beam glanced off something pale, a stark contrast to the darkness pressing in around him. Backtracking with the LED bulb, the glow again illuminated the object. As Detective Shaw bobbed in the water, staring at the grinning skull before him, he felt oddly calm.

*****

Carly stared out the sliding glass door into the growing dark beyond. "The clouds are thick tonight. It's going to be dark soon." Turning to Michelle, she said, "That's great news for us. Give me your phone."

"Huh? Why? No."

Carly eyed her warily as she walked to a hutch built into the wall behind Michelle. Opening a drawer, she pulled a gun out and held it aimed at Michelle as she crossed back to the door, saying, "Now I see where your sister got her sass from. Does it look like you're in a position to argue? Your phone. Now."

"My sister? You . . ."

"Yeah, I did. The little snoop came around asking questions about the neighbor's damn dog."

"Sunshine," Michelle whispered.

"What?"

"That was the dog's name. Sunshine."

"Yeah? Well now it's Freckle or Pickle or some dumb shit like that."

"The dog's not dead?"

"No. Listen." Carly sighed heavily, pursed her lips and rolled her eyes. "I didn't want to cause any trouble. I just wanted some peace and quiet, so I found someone who would come and take the damn barker away. But then your sister came around and started asking questions. I couldn't afford to have anyone else come looking into my business."

"Because then they'd know that Mrs. Burke didn't sell you this house. You took it."

"Yeah, I did. And I take those nice little checks she gets from Social Security every month, too. It's a sweet little deal, and I wasn't about to let some dumb kid ruin it all for me. Or her sister. Now give me your phone."

Michelle glared at the woman, not moving.

"Damn it!" In a flash Carly closed the distance between them, hitting Michelle on the temple with the gun, then pinning her head to the table with the muzzle. Waves of nausea washed over Michelle as she struggled to stay conscious, focusing on the pinpoint of light at the center of her blackening vision. When she recovered, she found herself seated in the chair again, hands bound behind her back. Lifting her head, she saw Carly by the door, again peering out into the night. She held both the gun and Michelle's cell phone.

"Oh, good. Tell me if this sounds like you. 'I blame myself. I'm sorry.' Or are you more of a 'Goodbye, cruel world' type?"

"What?"

"It doesn't matter. Suicide notes are strange. I'm sure suicide texts are even stranger. Now get up."

Slipping the phone into the back pocket of her pants, she yanked Michelle to her feet. Taking hold of Michelle's bound wrists, she pulled her towards the door, slid the glass panel back and pushed Michelle through.

"Now march."

Michelle stumbled across the lawn, weak and dizzy. Her feet sunk deep as Carly forced her closer to the marshy edges of the pond.

"Now kneel."

"What are you planning to do?"

Carly put the sole of her shoe against the backs of Michelle's knees and pushed. Michelle's knees sank into the chilly water at the pond's edge.

"That's up to you, girlie. Behave and you get to drown, see what your sister went through. Struggle and I shoot you in the head. Either way, I untie you, send the text to your parents, you're dead by suicide, and I can go back to my quiet little slice of luxury."

Michelle parted her lips to scream for help, only to find her head shoved roughly into the water. She started to struggle, flailing as much as she could with bound wrists, until she remembered what the woman had said. Either way, she was dead. She could experience what Amelia had in her last moments. There was a strange peace in that for Michelle.

She stopped fighting, holding her breath until she could resist no more, the pond water filling her mouth and nose, filtering into her lungs. A light entered at the edge of her vision. She gave herself over to the stream of thoughts flowing through her mind, a mix of memories and regrets. They melded together and began to spin, circling down the drain of her consciousness. Then she was on her side, violent spasms racking her body as she choked up what tasted like dirty turtle water.

Each cough radiated pain throughout her head. Her eyes seemed to scream under the blades of a dozen daggers as she opened them, tiny ripples of color spreading until the edges met, blurring together until her vision returned. What she saw made no sense. For a moment she thought it was a delusion, that she was still dying, or maybe this was death. Then the slick black figure that straddled Carly's back, pinning her to the ground, removed the odd beak from his mouth and pulled off his goggles.

"Michelle, it's Detective Shaw. Are you alright?"

Michelle felt such an intense elation about being here, in this moment, alive, that it took her a moment to turn her focus from Detective Shaw's face to his words.

"I need you to go and get help. I need you to call nine-one-one. Can you do that?"

Michelle pushed herself up to her hands and knees. She tried to talk, but her throat was swollen too tight to let words out. She sat back on her feet and nodded.

"Good girl."

Michelle found her balance and stood, her eyes still on Detective Shaw's, blue even in the dark. She couldn't leave yet. There was something else she needed.

"You got her, Michelle. You did it. You did a good job, but it's over. You've gotta leave the rest to me."

Nodding, Michelle moved, staggering in the direction of her house. She shivered, bittersweet tears springing to her burning eyes. She wondered if this would be enough, catching the woman who murdered her sister, or if she would spend the rest of her life battling against the darkness her sister's loss had seeded inside of her, doing, in essence, what had led to her sister's death – searching for Sunshine.

Searching For Sunshine first appeared of *Heater Magazine*, in volume 4, # 12

A Note From The Author

Of all the many wonderful, amazing books out there, thank you so much for choosing to spend some of your precious time on this one! I hope you had as much fun reading these stories as I did writing them.

Did you know that reviews are the biggest gift you can give an author? I know review have a huge impact on how I choose which books to read, and I suspect I'm not the only one. It would mean the world to me if you took just one more moment of your time and left a review for *Detecting Fear* on Amazon, Goodreads, or your favorite place to leave reviews.

Until we meet again . . . Happy Reading!

About The Author

With degrees in Crime Scene Technology and Physical Anthropology, Florida author Shannon Hollinger hasn't just seen the dark side of humanity – she's been elbow deep inside of it! She finds writing to be a much cleaner way to spend her time than the autopsy suite. Most days it smells better, too. When she's not writing, you can find her reading, hiking alongside snakes and alligators, and playing butler to a demanding terrier. Her short fiction has appeared in a variety of magazines and anthologies. A stack of full-length manuscripts await publication.

To see where you can find more of her work, find her on social media, or to join her mailing list for the latest updates and a FREE short story, check out www.ShannonHollinger.com.

www.ingramcontent.com/pod-product-compliance
Lightning Source LLC
Chambersburg PA
CBHW070628130626
46555CB00006B/2479